Sarah's Surrender

Cheryl Wright

SARAH'S SURRENDER

Copyright ©2021 by Cheryl Wright

Small Town Romance Publications

ALL RIGHTS RESERVED

This is a work of fiction. Characters, places, and incidents are a figment of the author's imagination. Any resemblance to actual events, locales, organizations or people living or dead, is totally coincidental.

Dedication

To Margaret Tanner, my very dear friend and fellow author, for her enduring encouragement and friendship.

To Alan, my husband of over forty-nine years, who has been a relentless supporter of my writing and dreams for many years.

To You, my wonderful readers, who encourage me to continue writing these stories. It is such a joy knowing so many of you enjoy reading my stories as much as I love writing them for you.

Table of Contents

Chapter One

Forsaken Ridge, Montana–1880

Sarah Gleason stared out the window, rifle at the ready.

She didn't have the patience for this nonsense, and Jarrod Black knew it. Despite what her pa had told him, she would not marry a lowdown drunk like him. Just as well pa had passed on, or she would give him an earful.

With a bottle of the stinking brew he always drank, still in his hand, Jarrod moved even closer. She pulled the trigger, aiming for a fraction above his shoulder. Enough to scare him off and warn him not to try again. Too bad he moved at the wrong time, and she grazed him instead.

"What the…?" he shouted, although, in his drunken state, it sounded like more of a slur.

She smirked. Pa had taught her to shoot and taught her good. The fact that Jarrod moved as she pulled the trigger wasn't her fault. Besides, it served him right, coming after her like this.

As she reloaded, Sarah pondered that he fully deserved it. After all, no meant no. She had told him in no uncertain terms on several occasions that she wouldn't marry him. She had no intention of changing her mind.

She glanced up moments later, but the weasel was gone. Apparently, her warning shot did the trick. Still, she would put nothing past the polecat and carefully scanned the area, but he was nowhere to be seen. His ever-suffering horse stood tied to a tree not far away, so he had to be here somewhere. A shudder went through her. *What on earth was the drunken fool up to now?*

The sudden creaking of the floorboards behind her had her spinning around, but it was too late. He was almost on top of her. Before she knew it, Sarah's hands were pulled tightly behind her back, with no means to escape. Despite her constant screaming, Jarrod continued to restrain her.

"Let me go, you grubby…."

The gag he tied around her mouth muffled the words no lady should utter. If that wasn't bad enough, he covered her eyes, no doubt with another filthy rag, making Sarah cringe. With her still kicking and screaming, Jarrod somehow managed to drag her up onto his horse and ride into town despite his drunken state.

"You're gonna marry me," he slurred over and over as they rode. It was the longest ride of her life. Sarah flinched as he slurped from the bottle on their way to the preacher. Oh, she was certain that's where they were heading. He'd as much as told her so.

When his horse stopped, he let her go. Heart pounding, she hit the hard ground. No doubt she was bruised from head to toe, but she had more important things to worry about–like Jarrod forcing her to marry him. Sarah prayed for a reprieve. How the good Lord would manage to get her out of her dire situation, Sarah had no idea, but it was all she had to hang onto right now.

Suddenly there was running, then scuffling around her. She had no idea what was taking place with her eyes covered and trussed up like a turkey. Her heart pounded as she imagined the worst case scenario.

"You idiot, Jarrod. What were you thinking?" The voice was familiar, but in her panicked state, she couldn't place it.

She tried to crawl away, but it was impossible. Then, sensing someone standing over her, a fresh wave of fear engulfed her. *What was going on?*

The rag on her eyes was abruptly removed, and Sarah blinked at the sudden bright light. The rope restraining her hands was cut, and the gag untied. She was on her feet in record time, pushing and shoving the stupid fool. He was far too drunk to push back.

"I'm gonna marry my Sarah," he told the Marshal as he took another mouthful.

Marshal John Wilson studied her. "You all right, Miss Gleason? This one will spend at least a few days in the jailhouse. He's gone a bit far this time. Kidnapping is a big leap from harassment." He grabbed Jarrod by the arms. "It will be up to the judge as to what his punishment will be, but he should get jail time for this."

"Apart from a few bruises, I think I'm fine." Sarah brushed the dust and dirt off her skirt and pondered her future. One thing she did know—she needed to get out of town and fast. Somewhere Jarrod would never find her.

Sarah slumped on the top step of her pa's ranch house. Well, technically, it was no longer Pa's ranch house. Until his death, she had no idea the ranch was about to be taken out from under her. Pa was more concerned with his drinking than paying the mortgage, more's the pity.

Jarrod was his drinking buddy, which is how she became unofficially betrothed to the skunk.

If he was still here, Pa would get a scolding–he had no right to tell Jarrod she would marry him. If he was the last man left in the world, she still wouldn't marry the fool. Oh, there was a time she might have considered it. At least when they were teenagers, and she was infatuated with him. As the years rolled by, Jarrod had begun to show his true colors. The thought brought back bad memories.

Sarah had worked hard on the family ranch for as long as she could remember. She was up at the crack of dawn every day to milk the cows. Pa hadn't seemed to care squat about the ranch these past few years, not since Ma had passed on. He hadn't cared about much at all anymore. He even said as much when she took him to task.

Well, he got his wish. He'd had one too many at the Welcome Saloon in town, taunted one too many drunken cowboys, and that was that. With no workers left because there was no money to pay them, she was out herding the horses when Marshal Wilson arrived to give her the news.

The next day she discovered the ranch had been sold on account of Pa being behind with his payments. By months, not days. There was no way Sarah could find that kind of money, not without selling herself at the saloon. Not that she ever considered it, but it had been suggested by the sleazy owner. When he saw her reach for her rifle, he hightailed it out of there. She hadn't seen hide nor hair of the despicable varmint since.

She threw back the last of the near-cold coffee, pondering her future. There was little she knew how to do except ranching. *Maybe she could get a job on a ranch?* But Sarah knew better. No woman had ever been hired to work on a ranch except for the cook, and even then, they favored men. Apart from the other hired hands ogling the female workers, you needed to be physically strong. She might be used to working the ranch, but she didn't have muscles like them cowboys did.

One thing she knew for sure–she had to get away from Forsaken Ridge, more's the pity. She loved this place, had lived here all her life. Pa insisted it was time she married, said she couldn't stay a spinster all her life. If he hadn't gone and got himself killed, she probably would have remained on the ranch for the rest of her days and been glad to do so.

The last thing she wanted was to marry, and she told pa so, but he brushed her concerns aside. In hindsight, he probably knew the ranch was about to be taken out from under them. If she wasn't still fuming from being kidnapped, she would be furious with her father, who'd only been buried a few days.

She stared out over their property. Well, the bank's property now. How could she leave this place? She'd been born here, and her mother had died here. Pa had died in this town too, only under far more dubious circumstances.

Sarah sighed. Dredging up old memories wouldn't help anyone. She likely only had a few days before that kidnapping polecat was released from the jailhouse, depending on how long it took for the judge to arrive. Besides, she couldn't count on the judge locking him away for much longer–he was, after all, Jarrod's cousin three times removed and always got the miserable fool out of every scrape he ever got himself into, which was often.

No, she had to get away and had to do it fast. There were only a few options available to her, especially given the time frame she was working with. Three days, or maybe a week at most, before that lowdown skunk, Jarrod Black, was released again.

Was that enough time to become a mail-order bride?

Helena, Montana–Four Days Later…

The lobby of the famous *Homestead Inn* was cozy, reminding her of the parlor of one of those fancy places she'd seen in the newspaper back home.

Sarah was in awe of her surroundings. The plush carpets and velvet covered chairs had her admiring the setting.

She couldn't help but glance about and was amazed at the intricate carvings on the ceiling. It set her mind to wondering about the accommodations. They must be luxurious. There would be beds a body could sink into and pillows that weren't made of hay. She could only dream about the warmth of the blankets and imagined walking barefoot on the plush carpets each room must possess. Not that Sarah would ever experience that kind of opulence. It was not the sort of thing she would ever be privy to.

She stared as one of the many butlers carried a tray of sparkling beverages to a small group of businessmen, and was envious of their wealth. She quickly admonished herself. It was not a very Christian thought, and she knew it.

She was suddenly pulled out of her thoughts as her companion spoke.

"I totally understand, Miss Gleason." Edna Crookshank nodded, exuding confidence with every word she spoke. Sarah sat opposite the older woman and studied her. She appeared to be in her mid-fifties, but Sarah couldn't be certain. One thing she did know was this woman, who was short of stature, knew what she was doing. Mrs. Crookshank and her matrimonial agency, *Western Mail Order Brides Agency*, had come highly recommended.

Well, if you could call an article in the local newspaper a recommendation. The article, which was an expose on the owner, mentioned Mrs. Crookshank hand-picked and personally interviewed both parties when possible. She also demanded references from the local preacher and sheriff, at the very least. Sarah still couldn't believe she was considering becoming a mail-order bride, but if she had to do it, and she did, then at least she knew she would be perfectly matched to her potential groom. "It was pure luck I was passing through Helena," she said. "My assistant telegraphed to say you were here."

"That *was* lucky." Sarah had been surprised to get such a quick result, and now she knew the reason. She'd fully expected to have to hide out here for some weeks. By that time, her meager savings would be gone. "I need to get out of here quickly. I don't even know if Jarrod is still in jail," she said, a scowl on her face. "His cousin the judge is as much an evil doer as Jarrod himself." She felt anger climbing its way through her entire being and tried to calm herself.

Mrs. Crookshank leaned forward and covered Sarah's hand with her own. "He's still there. My sources tell me the judge won't be along for another day or two at least."

"Tea for two." They were interrupted by the waitress, placing a silver tray on the low table between them before removing each item carefully. "And carrot cake for two, as you requested, Mrs. Crookshank."

"Thank you, my dear." The waitress quickly moved away, leaving them alone again. "Shall I pour?"

Sarah nodded. Never in her life had she been amid such luxury. Oh, she'd seen pictures for sure, but never in her wildest dreams did she expect to be sitting in such an expensive hotel. It was a stark difference to Woody's Saloon, where she was staying, with its bare floors and threadbare sheets. The comings and goings at all hours was off-putting, but sadly, it was all she could afford.

"I do have a match for you," the other woman told her as she pulled an envelope out of her high-priced reticle. "He's a rancher who owns a big spread. What he really wants is a cook and housekeeper, but propriety demands otherwise. Besides, he wants an heir." Mrs. Crookshank winked at her.

How the man expected an heir without marrying, Sarah had no idea. She rolled her eyes.

"What you mean is he wants a slave." As the words left her lips, Sarah knew she was being ungrateful. After all, who was she to make demands? She was in a precarious situation, and as Ma always said, beggars can't be choosers. Right now, she was a beggar who had been lucky to get away with a few of her meager possessions. They mostly consisted of her well-worn and nearly threadbare clothes. Currently, she was safely hidden from her kidnapper, and for that, she should be thankful. Sarah chewed at her lip. "I'm sorry, Mrs. Crookshank. I sound like an ungrateful wench. Pa always said I was, so I guess that proves it."

"Nonsense. And you must call me Edna." She leaned forward again, this time squeezing Sarah's hand. *If there wasn't a table between them, would Edna have hugged her?* Sarah seemed to think she might. "Shall I tell you about your potential groom?" She took her spectacles from her lap, placed them on her face, then opened the envelope. "Mr. Carson, Luke Carson, is a highly respected rancher. He is thirty-two years old and lives about twenty miles out of Carson's Hollow." She glanced at Sarah over the rim of her spectacles. "Sounds pretty good so far, eh?"

Sarah nodded in agreement.

"His local pastor gave him a glowing review, as did the sheriff. Unfortunately, I was unable to interview Mr. Carson myself, but I had one of my agents talk to him. From all accounts, I believe he would be perfect for you." She folded the letter and handed it to Sarah, along with the envelope it came in. "He is a man of means, and you would have a good life with Mr. Carson. I doubt you will ever want for anything."

"Thank you," Sarah said quietly, unsure of what else to say. *After all, what choice did she have?*

"Well, drink your tea, and eat up." Edna reached for the beautifully decorated China cup that sat in front of her. "Where are you staying, my dear?"

Sarah suddenly stopped with her cup mid-air. *Did she dare admit it?* "At Woody's Saloon," she mumbled.

Edna's eyes widened in surprise. "That will never do; it's far too dangerous." She beckoned the extravagantly dressed concierge and waited for him to arrive. "We need a room for Miss Gleason, please. Two nights at least, possibly more, depending on when the stage is coming through town."

Sarah was aghast. She could barely afford to stay at Woody's, let alone the outrageously expensive *Homestead Inn.* "But I can't…."

"It will all be taken care of by your groom, so don't worry yourself about it." Edna glanced at Sarah's thread-bare gown. "Tomorrow, we will go into town and outfit you." Sarah wore the only decent dress she owned, her Sunday best, as she wanted to put her best foot forward. Unfortunately, even her best didn't give the greatest impression. "Mr.

Carson expects his bride to arrive fully outfitted and ready to live as the wife of a wealthy rancher."

She couldn't allow this extravagance–what would her groom say?

"If you're worried about the cost, don't. Mr. Carson sent a very generous allowance to ensure you look the part."

Look the part. The more Sarah learned, the more it sounded as though he wanted his bride to play a role, as though she were an actress on the stage. Well, if that's what he wanted, and it kept her safe, who was Sarah to disagree?

"I'll do it." Her heart pounded. She was going in feet first with absolutely no idea of what would happen.

Edna grinned at her, then pulled some papers out of her traveling bag. "You'll need to sign this contract," she said, digging into her bag again for a pen. The concierge was suddenly by her side.

"Would this help, Madam?" A gold-lined fountain pen sat on a small silver platter. "Only the best for our guests," he quipped when Sarah gaped.

Edna took the proffered pen and handed it over to Sarah. She stared at the object; she'd never seen one before.

"It has its own built-in inkwell, Madam," the concierge stated, then left them alone.

"It's a new invention," Edna whispered, which helped soften her embarrassment.

Sarah glanced at the contract, then carefully signed her name at the bottom. She had attended school until she was twelve. Then with no sons available, she was put to work on the ranch. Her handwriting wasn't the best, but she could read and write. Not that she'd had much practice.

She handed the fountain pen back to Mrs. Crookshank, leaned back, and sighed. If it wasn't for her pa, she wouldn't be in this predicament, nor would she be hiding from Jarrod Black. And she definitely wouldn't have just signed her life away to become a mail-order bride.

Chapter Two

Sarah's eyes fluttered open. Today was the day she would leave Helena for her new home. She still couldn't believe she'd spent the past three nights in the luxurious *Homestead Inn*. All her meals were provided, and the butler she'd been assigned couldn't do enough for her. Mrs. Crookshank had accompanied her to the *Helena Boutique*, and her new wardrobe of clothes, including three pairs of boots, had been delivered two days ago, along with a traveling trunk fit for a Queen. There was also a new carpetbag to replace her threadbare one.

Her hair had been styled by the inn's exclusive stylist, and she'd been given a facial massage, the likes of which she'd never seen before. It was a once-in-a-lifetime opportunity, and she was so glad to have experienced it. She did, however, worry about the cost to her groom, wealthy or not.

Edna Crookshank had left yesterday for her ultimate destination. She had paid the account in advance and left specific instructions for Sarah to follow. The stagecoach would arrive at precisely 10.15, and Sarah must wait in the stage office out of sight. The concierge had arranged for her luggage to be collected and delivered to the stage office, so Sarah didn't have to worry about such trivial problems.

Mrs. Crookshank was an organized woman who had everything under control. Sarah could see why the *Western Mail Order Brides Agency Matrimonial Agency* was so popular and successful.

It was still early, and she had plenty of time to wash, dress, and go to the dining room for breakfast. Since everything had been paid upfront, she saw no reason not to take advantage of it. In the scheme of things, Carson's Hollow wasn't that far away. Tomorrow morning she would arrive at her destination, meet and marry Luke Carson, her groom-to-be. A shiver fluttered down her spine at the thought. What would he be like, this Luke Carson?

As a young girl, she had dreamed of one day marrying the perfect man. Someone she was madly in love with, and he with her. He would be handsome and tall and would have bulging muscles, as all the romance novel heroes did. Once she began working on the ranch, those dreams had faded into oblivion. Pa told her they were nothing but fantasies anyway and to stop wasting time on daydreams. It broke her heart.

As she descended the extravagant stairs toward the dining room, she felt like a princess. Her new gown fit perfectly, and the boots were so comfortable, Sarah felt like she was walking on air for the first time in her life. For as long as she could remember, she'd worn hand-me-downs. Not that it had ever bothered her before, but Mrs. Crookshank had treated her like she was someone special. Someone worth spending money on, and Sarah wanted to believe her.

She only hoped Luke Carson believed it, too. Would he be tall and handsome? She truly hoped he was like the man of her dreams all those years ago. It would complete the fairytale she was living now. Deep in her heart, she knew all of that could fall in a heap the moment she stepped off the stagecoach. If he didn't like her, or worse still, he didn't want her because of Jarrod, what then? *Would he make her pay back the money he had spent on her?* It wasn't a small sum—far from it. Sarah's heart thudded, and she stopped suddenly. It would be her worst nightmare. There was no way she could ever pay back such an overgenerous amount. Not in her entire lifetime.

Jarrod stalking and kidnapping her was bad enough, but how would she repay all the money Luke Carson had paid to make her presentable as his wife? A shiver went down her spine, and memories of the saloon owner's visit sent a shudder through her.

"Are you all right, Miss Gleason?" The concierge's voice brought her out of her dark thoughts. She glanced up and noticed he was waiting at the bottom of the stairs for her.

She put a false smile on her face. "Thank you, Mr. Jenkins. I'm fine. Just thinking is all."

He gave her the biggest smile, which warmed her heart. She knew it was his job, but the man always managed to lift her spirits. "Good to hear. Your table in the dining room is ready." He held her hand as she came down off the bottom step. "I will send someone up to your room shortly to deal with your luggage."

And just like that, her heart filled with joy. Sarah suddenly knew everything would turn out all right.

Carson's Hollow, Montana – the next day

Luke Carson paced the boardwalk as he waited for the stagecoach to arrive. How he allowed himself to be talked into this nonsense, he would never know. He needed a cook and housekeeper, for goodness sake, nothing more. Well, that wasn't entirely true–he needed an heir to the Carson fortune.

No man would bring himself down to the level of cleaning houses, and propriety being the way it was, he couldn't have a live-in lady without compromising both their reputations, so a wife it would have to be. Why did people always have to assume the worst?

Besides, his sister insisted it was past time he had an heir to his property. Why it was her problem, he'd never know. She lived in another state, for goodness' sake, and he hadn't seen her for two years. No, wait. He hadn't seen Maddy since she'd married four years ago, but they did keep in contact by mail. Maddy was a force to be reckoned with despite the distance between them, and he didn't dare go there. He pulled out his pocket watch and checked the time. Fifteen minutes late already–he hoped his bride had nothing to do with that. He could not abide tardiness. He also hoped she was attired correctly. He was a stickler for presentation.

Another thing Maddy annoyed him about–his insistence on looking the part. Just the thought of it had Luke straightening his tie. Or maybe he was secretly loosening it. He only knew a suit seemed appropriate to meet his bride, especially when he'd arranged to go straight to the church for them to be married. *He couldn't take an unmarried woman back to his home, could he?*

Luke glanced up and noticed wisps of dust up ahead. It wasn't long before he saw and heard the horses coming around the bend and heading for town. He hoped Miss Gleason, Sarah, would like Carson's Hollow. It was, after all, where he was born and had lived his entire life.

The horses slowed, and his heart pounded. Today would be life changing, not only for him but for his bride-to-be. He knew little of her background but was told she was in a desperate situation. Truth be told, Luke was too. He'd already had some of his men walk because there was no cook. His long-timers were forever loyal, but his most recent workers were young and knew nothing of loyalty. *More fool them.* Luke paid far more than most ranchers in the area for a good reason–he only employed the best. Of course, he expected them to come crawling back once they found out about his new cook. Er, his bride.

He glanced up again to see the stagecoach slowing. A young woman with dark brown hair stared out the window at him. *Was this his bride?* She looked petrified. Was she worried about marrying him or about becoming a mail-order bride? Both would be equally terrifying, he guessed. It was hard enough for him, but women were far more vulnerable and would have no clue what they were getting themselves into. He would do his best to be especially kind to her. Besides, if he didn't, Maddy would rip right into him.

The stagecoach finally stopped, and the driver climbed down, placing the steps in front of the carriage door. The young woman, who had been staring out the window, was the first to alight. She seemed about to burst into tears. *Was she his bride?* He took a deep, restorative breath. If it was Sarah Gleason, he needed to ensure she wasn't being forced into this marriage. The last thing he needed was to marry her, only to have her abscond soon afterward. That would leave him with a mess to clean up later.

Once everyone had alighted, Luke searched out his wife-to-be. "Miss Gleason. Miss Sarah Gleason?" He stood back a few steps and waited for one of the women to respond.

The woman's head shot up, and she stared at him. "Mr. Carson?" She seemed terrified of her own shadow, but she was pretty. In fact, she was beautiful. He looked her up and down. Her hair was in disarray, and her expensive gown creased, but that was to be expected after the distance she'd traveled to get here. She also looked incredibly tired.

"Do you have Miss Gleason's luggage, Matt?" he asked the driver. A large trunk and carpetbag were placed at his feet. Thank goodness he'd had the foresight to bring the wagon. Otherwise, he'd have had to make another trip into town to collect her belongings. Luke had asked Mrs. Crookshank to ensure his bride was properly attired but hadn't set a limit on how much she would need. "Thank you, Matt," he said as he picked up the trunk and placed it on the back of his wagon. He then reached for what appeared to be a brand-new carpetbag. It made him wonder about his bride that she required new bags. Where had she come from, and what were her living conditions like? Most importantly, what was the situation that had brought her to him? Mrs. Crookshank had been particularly guarded about that.

He also wondered if Miss Sarah Gleason could adapt to living on an isolated ranch such as his.

Until now, they hadn't spoken a word to each other beyond confirming they were the person each was looking for. But, if they were to marry, that would have to change. When he returned from the wagon, Luke noticed Sarah staring longingly at the signage for the bathhouse. He could have kicked himself. She had traveled a long way to get here and probably craved a hot bath and clean clothes. That was a request he could gladly fill.

Luke waited on the wooden seat outside the bathhouse. He'd helped Sarah retrieve a change of clothes from the trunk and taken her inside, where he paid the few coins it cost. If that's all it took to make his bride happy, he would be a lucky man indeed.

It felt like forever before she came out again, but it was worth the wait. The tired lines on her face had disappeared and were replaced with rosy cheeks. The fresh gown she wore brightened up her entire demeanor. She was even smiling as she came outside. "Feel better?"

"I do, thank you." She carried the carpetbag, which held her soiled clothes. Luke took it from her and led Sarah to their wagon across the street.

"If you're up to it now, we'll go straight to the church and see if the pastor is available." Her smile quickly disappeared. "Is something wrong, Sarah?" She didn't answer but instead chewed on her bottom lip. His suspicions seemed to be confirmed. "Are you being forced into this marriage?" His gaze didn't move from her face as he tried to fathom what was going on. "Because if you are…."

"No!" She answered quickly this time, which made him believe she was telling the truth. "It's not that," she whispered, her head down, eyes focused on the ground. "It's something else entirely. I need to tell you something important before we can contemplate getting married."

"Tell me what?" Now he was worried. *What exactly was he supposed to know?*

"Can we go somewhere private?" She looked worried, perhaps even upset. Luke linked his arm through Sarah's and headed toward the church. You couldn't get more private than that.

He'd listened carefully and hadn't said a word while she spoke. Tears rolled down her face as she explained the events of the past few weeks, and it took all his effort not to reach for her and hug Sarah tight. They weren't married yet, and he would be assuming a lot to do so. He held himself back with great difficulty. Pastor Petrie waited up at the front while they talked, willing to step in and marry them if or when they decided to go ahead.

Luke was of two minds; he didn't like being pushed into marriage, which is what his sister Maddy had done to him. But, on the other hand, Sarah, his betrothed, needed protection. Marrying her would be a big step toward protecting her as she would have a change of name.

In addition to all of that, Luke Carson was a man of his word. He had promised to marry Sarah Gleason, and that's exactly what he would do. So he stood, pulling her up with him. "Ready to get married?"

She stared at him, eyes wide. "You still want to marry me?"

"I promised, didn't I? You've been truthful with me, and I can't ask for more than that." He knew he shouldn't but pulled her into his arms. She was trembling, and he held her tighter. His arms enveloped her, and it felt as though they'd been together forever. He rubbed a hand across her back, and soon the quivering stopped. "Ready?" he whispered, and she nodded.

They walked to the front of the church, arm in arm, and soon they were husband and wife.

His ranch was about an hour out of town, but this trip seemed to take far longer than ever before. Perhaps it was the silence between them, but Luke was almost certain it was the unknown. Would that fool man come looking for his wife, and if he did, what was he likely to do? Of course, Luke could employ a hired gun to stand guard on the place, but that seemed like he'd be inviting trouble.

They finally came to the archway that heralded the *Carson's Hollow Ranch* entrance, and he brought the horses to a stop. The name had been etched long before Luke was born. In fact, even before his father had entered the world. His grandfather, his namesake, Luke Carson, had begun this ranch with only a small pocket of land. He'd saved every penny to expand his property and did so every time land was up for sale, and he had enough saved. He refused to go into debt for expansion, and for that, Luke would be eternally grateful.

"Carson's Hollow Ranch?" She arched her brows. "Like the town?"

"Both named after my grandfather, Luke Carson."

"That's wonderful. I love family history."

Apart from when they talked in the church, they were the most words Sarah had said to him since she arrived. "Well, not far to go now. As you can see, the property is extensive. That dot in the distance is the ranch house." He flicked the reins, and the horses began to move again.

She stared at the dot for a long moment. Did she think it would be a tiny cottage? Luke hoped she was in for a surprise. "I should have told you this before," she said, turning to face him. "I…I'm not the greatest cook. But I can cook."

He let out a long breath. For a moment, he wondered what was coming. Compared to her first confession, this was nothing. "My men will be glad for anything they don't have to cook themselves. We've mostly been living on beans and bacon, as well as eggs. I have a large brood of hens, so eggs are aplenty."

She smiled briefly. "I can do better than that, so I guess that's a bonus."

His heart fluttered. Sarah's smile lit up her face, and he wished she would smile more often. Her worry over her stalker was undoubtedly the reason, but he hoped being married to him would make her happy. *Was he being selfish? Or even self-centered?* Luke wasn't sure, but he knew that despite knowing her for only a matter of hours, his goal was to make his wife very happy to be married to him.

He reached across and covered her hand, squeezing it gently. A shiver went up his arm. Instead of pulling his hand away as he was inclined to do, he brought her hand to his lips and kissed it. This time, a tingle went down his spine. She turned to stare at him, and Luke wondered if she felt that too.

He mentally shook himself. It was crazy even to think it. They were complete strangers who had married for different reasons. There was no rhyme or reason for the things he felt, and no doubt it was all in his imagination.

They finally arrived at the ranch house. It was quite large compared to most in the area, as his grandfather had built it with family and future generations in mind. However, despite its age, the building was in good condition. His father had always ensured repairs were done quickly when needed, and Luke had done the same.

He glanced across at his new bride. Her jaw had dropped, and her eyes opened wide in wonderment. Warmth spread through him at her reaction. Luke climbed down from the wagon and moved to her side to help her down. She started to climb down herself, but as her husband, that was his job. He glanced up at her, placing his hands carefully on her waist. She looked down into his face and smiled.

He slowly lifted her down; a flutter went through him. As he slowly lowered her toward the ground, his eyes focused on her lips. She was such a temptation this new wife of his, and despite his best attempts to resist, he swooped in and quickly kissed her lips. She gasped, and then her smile returned.

Luke's hands were still around her waist, and if he was honest with himself, he didn't want to move them. He liked touching her–he knew he shouldn't, but he couldn't deny it. He'd planned on a marriage of convenience, consummating the marriage only for the purpose of producing an heir. Not that he'd told Sarah that, but now, since he'd met her, his mind was a jumble. She was so pretty, and so… wonderful. The total opposite of what he had expected.

He had decided long ago that the only women who would apply to be a mail-order bride would be old hags. Even his foreman had told him that. Worse still, Luke had believed it. All that had changed since he'd collected his wife. She was the farthest thing from a hag you could get. Sure, she had her problems, but her looks and personality were not amongst them.

Her hands sat on his shoulders, and she stared into his face. "Are we going inside, or shall we stand here all day?"

Her words brought him out of his thoughts, and he led her up the steps to the house. Luke unlocked the front door, then swooped in and carried her across the threshold. When he glanced at her, Sarah looked shocked, as though she hadn't expected it. Well, she was his bride, and every bride should have the memory of being carried across the threshold by her groom. Maddy had ensured he knew it, too.

When he stepped inside, her arms around his neck, Luke was reluctant to put his bride down. He liked the way he felt when they touched. He'd loved the way a shiver went through him when he'd stolen that kiss earlier, and wanted to do it again. Her hand reached up, caressing his cheek, and a shudder went through his entire body. Luke decided getting married was dangerous, for his heart, that was. He had previously decided to keep his distance from his wife. To not get emotionally involved, he'd even made a decision to place her in a spare room away from his own.

Now he wasn't so sure. Sarah Gleason, or Carson as she now was, had already got under his skin and into his heart. In just a few hours, she had changed his mindset and his life. What would happen after they'd been together for a month or more?

He dared not even think about it.

Sarah stood with her back to the kitchen countertop. *Mack, George, Roy, Pete, Colt, and Hank.* She repeated the names over and over in her head. Since she would be cooking for these men on a daily basis, she needed to learn their names. Right now, though, the only name she really wanted to know was Luke, her new husband.

Last night he'd made her his wife in every way. She hadn't expected that, and he'd even suggested he didn't want a proper wife, but he did need an heir. Isn't that what Mrs. Crookshank had also told her?

Along the way, something changed. It had for her too. If Sarah recalled correctly, something had shifted in her when he'd carried her across the threshold. A shiver had run through her at his touch, and when she'd caressed his cheek, Luke's demeanor had changed. Hers too. She had suddenly wanted more than a marriage of convenience; she wanted the whole shebang, a real husband, and a brood of children to go with it. When he'd placed her on the floor, instead of stepping back as she'd expected him to do, he pulled her closer then kissed her. Sarah had never been kissed like that before, and she felt warmth travel through her. Luke swooped her up again and carried her into the bedroom, their bedroom, and she soon became Mrs. Luke Carson in every way.

"Thank you, Missus, for a delicious breakfast." Sarah's thoughts were interrupted, and she glanced up at Mack, Luke's foreman.

"You are welcome, Mack. What time should I expect you for lunch? Noon, or later?"

"Noon would be good, Missus." Mack nodded slightly, then headed for the door, snatching up his well-worn hat on his way out.

One by one, the men all stood and thanked her. It was far more than she'd ever had on pa's property. That lot was rough and ready, and if she hadn't stood her ground, given half a chance, each and every one of them would have ruined her. Luke's arms came up around her, and Sarah turned to face him. Leaning against him, she could hear his heartbeat, and it warmed her heart. Becoming a mail-order bride was a big concern to her, especially after her dealings with Jarrod. What if she'd married another drunkard? It had been her biggest worry.

As it transpired, she need not worry. Her husband was a caring man who had been gentle with her on their first night together. She sighed as she leaned against him. His arms enveloped her, and she didn't want him to leave. Staring up at him, knowing he must go, made her sad, which was crazy given they'd known each other for less than a day.

Luke's hand came up, and he lifted her chin and leaned in to kiss her. Sarah didn't complain. "I have to go," he whispered. "More's the pity. I could easily stay and get lost in those eyes." He kissed her again, but this time it was a far less passionate kiss than before. Oh, she knew the reason; he had work to do, and it was far too enticing to stay. She felt exactly the same way.

He pulled away but held tight to her hands, as though it was the hardest thing in the world for him to leave. Luke was a handsome man, although perhaps a little rough around the edges. He was unshaven and needed a good haircut, but he was everything she'd imagined a husband to be. He was at least six feet tall, her head only reached his shoulder, and every time she glanced into his face, she got lost in his chocolate-colored eyes.

He turned to walk away, but she called him back. "Wait! I made muffins for the men." She shoved a calico bag into his hands. "For later." His smile lit up his face, and a shiver went down her spine. Was it the man himself or his approval that made her feel so good? She thought perhaps it was a little of each. He leaned forward again and kissed her briefly on the forehead, then quickly retreated as though he didn't trust himself to stay any longer.

The moment Luke was gone, Sarah collected up the soiled dishes and placed them in the bowl used for that purpose. She grated soap into the bowl before adding the boiling water waiting on the stove. She wiped down the table and ensured the kitchen was clean and tidy before starting work on the thick vegetable soup she intended to prepare for lunch. Rising bread sat on the countertop – it would be quite some time before it was ready to be placed in the oven.

She was glad she'd insisted they stock up on food before they left town. She couldn't cook without decent supplies. Apart from some moldy bread and rancid butter, the pantry had been entirely bare when Sarah arrived but was now full of the essential items she would need on a daily basis.

She threw two handfuls of barley into a large pot, covered it with water, set it on the stove to boil, and then began chopping the rest of the ingredients. She'd picked up some vegetables from the mercantile since Luke wasn't sure the vegetable patch would even be viable—it was so long since anyone worked it. Sarah had noticed its overgrown state when she arrived and hoped it wasn't as bad as it looked.

With the soup now cooking, she made a batch of pastry for an apple pie. She'd bought enough of the fruit for at least two pies, as she was sure it would keep the men happy. After all, they couldn't be expected to work unless their bellies were full. She'd learned that very early in her life.

She stirred the soup and breathed in the aroma. It sure did smell good. There was nothing better than the scent of a kitchen full of food cooking. At least that's what ma always said, and Sarah agreed. She was comfortable in the kitchen; she'd been providing meals for cowpokes since she was a teenager. Ma had always done most of the cooking, but once she passed, the responsibility fell on Sarah. As she'd told her husband, she wasn't the best cook around, but she did all right and could satisfy an empty belly. Her first love was being out on the ranch, but the men had to be fed.

Chapter Three

With lunch now over, and the kitchen clean again, Sarah made herself a cup of tea before settling on the porch. Luke's property was huge–as far as she could see and beyond, all belonged to him. She sipped the tea taking in the large expanse, then shivered, realizing she was totally alone here at the ranch house.

As quickly as the thought came to her, she shook it away. Jarrod was in jail and couldn't get to her. *Or was he?* He certainly was a few days ago, but that meant nothing. To date, Judge Edgar Black had declined to incarcerate his distant cousin and instead constantly set him free to continue his reign of terror on Sarah, and indeed, anyone else he decided to intimidate. Because that was the main thing he'd been locked up for in the recent past, although there were several episodes of drunk and disorderly.

A shiver went down her spine, and when she glanced up, far into the distance, Sarah was convinced she saw a lone man standing, staring down at her. Her heart thudded, and panic engulfed her. Then she remembered Jarrod was safely locked away, and with any luck, would be for some years. Her imagination was playing games with her. It had to be. How would he even know where to find her? She shook herself. He wouldn't because she didn't even tell Sheriff Wilson where she was going. Heck, when she'd left, she didn't know where she was going herself.

Sarah closed her eyes and willed herself to calm down. Jarrod was nowhere near Carson's Hollow and did not know where she now lived. She was safe and would be for as long as she didn't return to Forsaken Ridge. But, when she opened her eyes again after her heart rate had slowed, he was gone. It made her wonder if Jarrod was ever there. She shivered and decided he was a cruel figment of her imagination.

Instead of dwelling on the fright she'd had, Sarah decided to look around. Luke hadn't really given her the tour he'd promised, and she had no idea where anything was except the pantry. Of course, she'd sought that out herself. Otherwise, everyone would have been starved of food by now. The thought made her smile. She couldn't imagine any of these hard-working men going without food.

She strolled into the kitchen with her now empty cup, where she washed and dried it. Sarah stared out the window over the sink. What was that in the distance? Was it a…? It certainly looked like a spring house, and her heart leapt with joy. What wonderful surprises would she find there? And why didn't her husband tell her about it? They had bought only basic supplies at the mercantile. So perhaps he'd planned on telling her later. Or perhaps he'd not given it a thought. It was the sort of thing men would think of as women's business.

She sighed. More than likely, she was correct. Sarah wondered how long it had been since the small structure had been used. Was the spring even running? She hadn't noticed water of any description as they'd arrived. On the other hand, she was exhausted, not only from the travel but from the fear Jarrod had inflicted on her, but trying to keep herself hidden as well. She decided to check it out for herself and headed outside.

She might have already dismissed the possibility of Jarrod turning up unannounced, but she stood at the front door and stared into the distant surroundings. Happy there was no one to be seen, she continued toward the spring house. Sarah couldn't believe her luck in marrying a man of means such as Luke. Unfortunately, there was no spring house on her pa's property, but they did have a root cellar. She hadn't found one here yet, but she was confident there would be a root cellar attached to the ranch house; she would look for it later.

As she approached the door to the outside room, she glanced about, ensuring she was truly alone. The last thing she needed was to be cornered inside such a small structure. Her hand on the door handle, Sarah tried to tug it open, but the door wouldn't budge. How long had it been since it had been used? Quite a while, by the look of things. Not one to be beaten, she persisted, and finally, it moved, then eventually opened. She stepped inside, and a shiver went through her. Was it the coolness of the spring house that made her shiver, or was it the ghosts of Luke's ancestors? Perhaps they were telling her she didn't belong here.

Sarah wished she'd brought a shawl with her to chase away the crisp, cold air. She fought the overwhelming urge to shudder and instead slowly moved into the dark room, then stopped, letting her eyes acclimatize to the darkness. She could hear water running, and its calming sound reassured her. She glanced about and spotted a small box in the far corner. Her excitement at finding some hidden treasure had her scurrying over, but it was empty. There was nothing to be seen. Disappointment flooded her. How long was it since anything was stored in here?

"There's nothing here." She gasped at the sound of Luke's voice as it came suddenly out of nowhere. "I didn't mean to scare you," he said, moving closer to her. His arms came up around her, and Sarah felt reassured.

"I… I was just checking it out," she said, finally finding her voice. "In case there were food items in here."

His eyebrows suddenly shot up. "The spring house hasn't been used for at least a decade. My mother probably used it at some point, but I can't recall. I spent my days working the ranch." There was a twinge of bitterness in his voice, and Sarah completely understood. Offspring of ranchers were expected to work from a very young age. In many cases, it was the only way they survived.

She didn't say anything but nodded her understanding. Luke gazed into her eyes for long moments, as though there was something else he wanted to say. Or do. Without warning, he leaned in and kissed her lips. Sarah closed the short distance between them and found herself kissing him back. A soft groan escaped her lips, and Luke chuckled. "We could go into the house," he whispered against her ear.

"I thought I saw Jarrod on the hill earlier." Sarah suddenly pulled away, studying his reaction, but Luke gave nothing away. *Did he not believe her?*

"Are you certain," he asked in his slow drawl.

She wasn't and admitted as much. "It was probably my imagination playing tricks on me." It was difficult to concede, but Sarah was sure it was the truth.

He reached out and took both her hands. "He's in jail, so you're safe. I'll keep you safe either way." Luke leaned in and stole another quick kiss.

"What are you doing here, anyway?" It came out more like an accusation than a question, but it wasn't her intention. "I mean, did you need me for something?"

He led her out of the small building and closed the door behind them. "I came to check on you to make sure you were all right on your first day."

That sounded strange to Sarah since she'd seen him at lunchtime but didn't say so. "I can look after myself," she said more tersely than she'd intended, proving to Sarah she was more stressed than she realized. "I would like to know where you keep your rifle. Just in case." The shocked expression on Luke's face surprised her. "I can shoot, you know," she said abruptly as she stiffened.

Out of nowhere, he began to laugh. "Of course you can. What else can you do that I know nothing about."

Sarah pursed her lips and studied him through half-closed eyes. "I can do anything you can do," she ground out in a huff and hurried ahead of him.

"Sarah… I didn't mean…."

She didn't hear the rest as she turned the corner of the ranch house, but one thing was for sure–she had something to prove to her husband, and she sure as heck would do it.

~*~

Luke did his best to be a loving husband and a protector, but he couldn't be with Sarah every minute of the day. Instead, he made sure she knew where the house rifle was kept and that it was loaded. Not that he expected she would need to use it. Better safe than sorry, his mother always said, and he thought it better to err on the side of caution for Sarah's sake.

She was still distant with him after his earlier foolishness. Laughing when she said she could shoot was utter idiocy on his part. Firstly, because he had no idea if it was true, and secondly, because of what he was experiencing right now. He was definitely in the doghouse and wasn't sure how long it would take to get back into his new bride's good books.

He'd learned his lesson for sure, and it wouldn't happen again. Supper was a cold and distant affair, and the glances he'd had from his workers didn't help either. He would get a good ribbing tomorrow, there was no doubt. One day married, and already he'd put his foot in it. On the other hand, he couldn't wait to find out what else she could do–if that was even true. Sarah was a beautiful woman, one other men would be envious of. He couldn't imagine her handling a firearm, let alone shooting something or even a person with one. It was almost laughable. A chuckle tried to force itself out of his mouth at the thought, but Luke stopped it before any further damage could be done.

The men sat at the supper table, finishing off their coffee. Sarah opted to do the dishes so she could rest for a while before retiring for the night. The way the night was going, Luke was certain she would sleep in the spare bed tonight – but not if he could help it. He wanted for them to get back on an even footing and back into the warm relationship they'd had prior to his stupidity.

"Thanks for supper, Missus." One by one, the men thanked her and headed for the bunkhouse. Normally they would hang around for a while and talk. It had been a long-time tradition dating back to his grandfather's time. Were they giving the newlyweds their space, or were they avoiding the cold atmosphere currently engulfing them? Either way, it was probably for the best right now.

Pushing back his chair, Luke swallowed down the last gulp of his coffee and strolled over to his wife. "I'm really sorry," he offered quietly as he came up behind her. She snatched up the coffee mug but said not a word. His arms came up around her waist, then he tugged her closer. "Forgive me?" He felt her stiffen in his arms and knew it wasn't a good sign.

"I *can* shoot, you know," she said between gritted teeth. "Pa taught me to shoot when I was five years old. Of course, Ma was not pleased, but my shootin' put food on the table more than once over the years." She spun around in his arms and stared into his eyes. "You should know a ranch kid can shoot, and ride, and do all the things a ranch kid needs to do." Now she glared at him.

"Boys, sure, but not a girl." He studied her–she didn't appear to be embellishing the facts.

"There was no boy to do it. I was the only surviving kid, much to pa's disgust." There was a sudden sheen to her eyes, and Luke regretted his interrogation. "*Two sons and a daughter, and only the daughter survives.* He always said that when he was mad at me. It cut through my heart back then, and all these years later, it still does."

Luke's heart thudded. What sort of father says such a thing to his child? *A cold-hearted fool, that's who.* He suddenly wanted to comfort her and pulled Sarah against his chest. At first, she resisted, being the stubborn woman she was, but she eventually gave in and leaned into him. "I'm really sorry," he whispered. "That was a terrible thing your father did."

"Stop being sorry. I'm a big girl. I can handle it." But Luke wasn't so sure. He saw those tears shimmering in her eyes, and when he glanced down, saw a tear trickle down her face. He wiped it away with his thumb, then gently kissed her forehead. His wife was not as strong as she pretended to be.

"From now on, you have me to lean on," he said quietly, meaning every word. "I will protect you and look after you."

"I can look after myself," she whispered.

A smile formed on his face. His wife sure was stubborn. "We'll be a team then."

When he glanced down at her, she was smiling. "I'm ready for bed," she said quietly, a coy look on her face. Luke picked her up and carried her to their marital bed. It was going to be all right after all.

Breakfast was well over, and once everyone had left, she decided to take a short break. Before anything else, she would double-check the rifle Luke kept in the closet, right near the front door. Check it was loaded and ready should she need to use it. It gave her some reassurance should Jarrod turn up unexpectedly.

There was so much to do to make this house a home, and she needed to get her mind off a figment of her imagination. Firstly she would sweep and wash all the floors, then she would see to the dusting. It was obvious a bachelor lived here; his desperate need for a housekeeper was now clear. Tomorrow, she would strip all the beds and wash the bedding.

More than anything, Sarah was desperate to get out on the ranch, to pitch in wherever she could. Not that she'd discussed it with Luke. She was sure he wouldn't approve. Except for their brief conversation at the spring house, not once had he asked what she did back home. Like most men, he probably assumed she would be the ideal wife, spending her time cooking and baking to fill the bellies of the cowpokes. Back home, in the end, there were no cowpokes. Pa had drunk every spare cent they had, and she'd had to let them go. Without Sarah working the land, they would have lost the ranch far earlier.

Looking back, that would have been preferable because then her pa might not have promised her to that lowdown polecat, Jarrod Black. Then she wouldn't be in the situation she was in right now—having to lower herself to become a mail-order bride and marry a total stranger.

Still, she could have done far worse. Luke seemed like a decent man. He'd treated her kindly so far and even seemed to like her, which suited Sarah fine since she liked him too. She hoped as time went on, they would become closer, and perhaps one day, he might even come to love her.

Sarah shook herself at the thought. That scenario was highly unlikely, and she knew it. Taking a mail-order bride was usually for at least one of two reasons; to have an unpaid cook and housekeeper or have a warm body in their bed to fulfill their manly needs. The thought of a loveless marriage filled her with dread.

Pulling her thoughts away from things she couldn't control or change, Sarah decided to check out the vegetable patch but needed to prepare biscuits first. She had two chicken pies ready to go in the oven and couldn't afford to keep the men waiting for their food. So she slipped the apron over her head and pulled out all the ingredients for biscuits. Once the mixture was ready, she sprinkled flour on the countertop, ready to roll it out.

She made two dozen biscuits, not sure how many she would need. Sarah had always been a hard worker, and things were no different now, but she was exhausted. Perhaps she was trying too hard to please her new husband? She needed a break. Five minutes would not hurt, surely? It was a pleasant day with a warm breeze blowing, and she decided to sit out on the porch. Sipping her tea, Sarah stared out into the distance. *What would Luke be doing right now?* Mending fences, catching cows that had strayed too far, or chasing mustangs? There were far too many scenarios to know for sure, but one thing was certain – she wished she was out there with him.

Wishing wouldn't make it happen, and for now at least, she was stuck here in the ranch house cooking biscuits and other treats for the men. She gulped down the last of her lukewarm tea and stood, ready to return to the kitchen. As she began to turn to go inside, Sarah glanced up once more, and there he stood. Jarrod Black was there in the distance. A little closer than the last time she'd seen him. Her heart raced, and she shook her head, trying to erase this imaginary man standing there, watching her.

But he didn't evaporate this time. This was not a figment of her imagination–Jarrod was standing there, she was certain this time. Sarah quickly headed inside and sprang toward the closet, snatching up the rifle in record time. She stood far enough back from the door that the fool could open it, but not so far he wouldn't see her the moment he entered. This wouldn't be the first time she'd fired a rifle, and it certainly wouldn't be the last. If it was Jarrod, she would have to move quickly, depending on how drunk he happened to be. Because he would be drunk, there was no doubt. She hadn't seen him sober for months.

She stood frozen to the spot and stiffened as she heard footsteps close by. "Stay where you are, or I'll blow your head off," she said far more confidently than she felt. As the door slowly opened, she cocked the trigger, making the man on the other side pause.

"Sarah, it's me!" Luke shouted, throwing the door open at the same time. *What on earth was his wife doing, aiming a rifle at him?*

She sighed in relief and lowered the firearm. Her face was devoid of color. She was shaking now, but as she'd held that rifle, her hands were steady. He stepped forward and enveloped her tightly.

"It's safe to come in," he called to his workers, who waited outside. What they would think, Luke had no idea, but his only concern right now was his wife.

"I, I saw Jarrod out there, and then when I heard footsteps on the porch…." She blinked rapidly as though trying to fight back the tears, and until that moment, he had no idea how truly scared she was. Luke motioned for the men to check, but he was confident there would be no one. They would have seen him on the way in here.

Why did he leave her alone? He should have stayed with her. At least ensure she felt safe with her new surroundings. If something did happen, she had no place to hide because she didn't know her way around. Luke silently admonished himself for his stupidity. If this Jarrod Black was as determined as Sarah said he was, he could well have been out there. *And if he was there today, what was stopping him from returning tomorrow?*

Luke already knew the answer–absolutely nothing.

From now on, someone would have to be in earshot of the house. Oh, he already knew Sarah wouldn't like it, but as her husband, Luke had a responsibility to protect her. He tightened his grip on his wife. "You're safe now," he whispered, and she suddenly pulled back.

"You think I can't protect myself?" She glared at him, hands on hips. "I've already shot that polecat once before."

Luke stared in disbelief. "You've shot him?"

"Yeah. More's the pity I only grazed his shoulder and didn't kill the drunken fool."

He looked down at the rifle held tightly in her hands. "Let me put that away." He reached for the firearm, but she was reluctant to let go. "There are seven men here willing to protect you. Besides, there's no one out there now."

"He was there, I know it. I saw him halfway up the hill. He was closer this time." He watched as defiance crept across her face.

It was so far in the distance, it was impossible to make out who was there, or even if someone was there. Was her imagination getting away with her? It was highly possible, but Luke wasn't fool enough to say so. It was clear his wife was terrified of this man, and that was the last thing she needed. The last thing he needed. A trip into town and a visit to the sheriff was definitely in order.

Chapter Four

Instead of spending the day doing laundry and cooking for Luke's workers, Sarah sat beside her husband on the buggy. They were on the outskirts of town and would visit with the sheriff soon. However, she would far prefer to be back at the ranch.

Still convinced Jarrod had visited the Carson's Hollow Ranch, Sarah was vigilant on their trip to town. She would put nothing past Jarrod and knew he was capable of anything that meant he would get his way. And that included riding out in front of them, guns blazing. She reached down under the seat of the buggy, reassuring herself Luke's rifle was right where she'd placed it. He turned toward her, raising his eyebrows. "You don't honestly think…."

"I do," she said forcefully. "Jarrod is like a fox in a hen house; you can't trust him." Luke didn't look convinced, but Sarah knew what he was really like. Unfortunately, it seemed Luke would find out for himself very soon.

They came to a halt outside the Sheriff's Office, and Sarah took a steadying breath. *Was she really going through this again?* The worst part was putting everyone else in danger. Jarrod had professed his love for her on many occasions, but not once did he prove that love. Not that she would have married him if he had. Oh no, that was never on her agenda. One drunkard in the family was enough, and look how that had ended for her father.

"Ready?" Luke stood on the boardwalk, staring up at her, his arms outreached and ready to help her down.

Was she ready? Sarah wasn't certain. She thought she'd put all this Jarrod nonsense behind her when she'd left Forsaken Ridge. But apparently not. She stared at her husband, then nodded. His hands felt nice on her waist, and when he lifted her down, all she wanted to do was lean into him and feel his strong arms around her. When she was safely on the ground, she reached for the rifle, and Luke frowned. "I don't think the sheriff will take too kindly to you lugging a rifle into his office. Might take it as some sort of threat."

She stared at him momentarily, and a shudder went through her. "Of course, I just…."

"I know," he interrupted, then put his arm to her waist and guided Sarah inside.

Inside, there was a wooden desk with a well-worn chair behind it—the desk was covered with papers, including several *Wanted* posters. The sheriff was nowhere to be seen. It wasn't long before she heard the clatter of cell doors, and the sheriff wandered out not long afterward.

"Luke Carson," Sheriff McKenzie Dunn said, a surprised look on his face. "What brings you out this way?" He stared at her curiously.

"This is my new bride, Sarah Carson. She was kidnapped by a man back in Forsaken Ridge and swears she saw him on my property yesterday." The look that passed between the two men was not lost on Sarah. Fury boiled up inside her, but, difficult as it was, she didn't say a word.

"Forsaken Ridge, eh?" Sheriff Dunn shuffled through the papers on his desk until he pulled out a *Wanted* poster. "Is this the man, Mrs. Carson?"

Sarah gasped and suddenly felt lightheaded. Luke helped her into a chair. "That's him. Does that mean he's not in jail? Did that fool cousin of his let him out again?" She would put nothing past Edgar.

"Judge Black took ill, and another judge was sent in his place. He gave Black two years, but he escaped on his way to the prison. Dang fool. When they catch him, he'll get more time."

"He escaped?" Her voice came out as a squeak letting everyone know just how stressed Sarah was.

"Yes, Ma'am, he did. Unfortunately, there's no proof he's out this way, although we believe he does know you're in Carson's Hollow."

"He knows? How can that be? I told no one." Sarah felt sick to her stomach and was in danger of losing her breakfast.

"His cousin, formerly Judge Edgar Black, found the information via marriage registration. He passed it onto his cousin. Judge Black is now awaiting trial."

She stared at him in disbelief. "I, I need some air," she bolted outside. Sarah gulped in the clean air but stayed close to the wagon and rifle. Out the corner of her eye, she saw someone peek around the corner of a building. At least that's what she thought she saw. She was even more wary now than before. Now she knew for certain Jarrod was out of jail, and more likely than not, he was trying to find her.

The door creaked behind her, and Luke appeared.

"He's here now, I'm certain," she said, scanning the immediate area. "I can feel his eyes on me." She could tell from the expression on his face that Luke thought she was overreacting. Only yesterday, he thought she had an overactive imagination. Perhaps now he would understand she wasn't making it up. Now he would know Jarrod was a real threat.

To all of them.

"The sheriff gave me a *Wanted* poster to show the men. We'll have to work out a plan." Sarah nodded but knew a plan would not work with Jarrod–he was far too unpredictable. "In the meantime, let's go to the diner and grab a bite to eat before we head back to the ranch. If there's anything else you need while we're in town, we can get that too." All Sarah wanted was to go back home where she felt reasonably safe. Right now, she felt like a sitting duck out in the open like this.

Then again, knowing Jarrod the way she did, he wouldn't shoot at them while they were out here. It was far too easy for him to be caught. He preferred to creep up on his prey and not let them know he was there. It was how he hunted animals for food, and it was the way he'd hunted her right before he'd kidnapped her.

"We should get inside somewhere. We'll head for the diner."

Sarah glanced across at Luke. "He won't go after me out here. Too easy–he prefers a challenge." She took her husband by the hand and strolled across Main Street toward the diner. If she was wrong,

Jarrod would pluck her off her feet in mere seconds. She tried not to think about it.

As the weeks passed, Sarah felt more and more comfortable with her new life on Carson's Hollow Ranch, despite several distant sightings of Jarrod. He kept his distance, and she was always the only one to spot him. It was as though he knew when Sarah would be alone. She was thankful the sheriff had been able to confirm the possibility of Jarrod being in the area as she now knew she wasn't imagining it.

"Good morning," Luke said, strolling into the kitchen. "How is my favorite girl today?" Sarah felt the heat rising up her face.

"I'm good." Before she had a chance to say more, Luke leaned in and kissed her passionately.

"I missed you this morning." His words made Sarah chuckle. She'd been up for less than thirty minutes. His arms firmly around her, she heard the front door open, which meant it was time to feed everyone. She tried to pull away, but Luke held her even tighter.

"I have to go," she whispered, but he was having none of it.

"They'll wait," he whispered back. "I'm enjoying holding my wife." He glanced down at her, a big grin on his face. Sarah was certain this was about possession, making sure everyone knew whose wife she was. Not that they needed telling. Each and every one of the cowpokes had been an absolute gentleman. Even on the rare occasion she'd been alone in the house with one or more of them.

They'd all been respectful toward her. It was as though Luke had warned them to keep their distance from his wife. She wouldn't put it past him to make certain the other men knew she was his wife and to treat her well. Not that Sarah expected anything else. She hadn't encountered even one incident where that hadn't happened.

"Hm, but the pancakes won't." She pulled out of his arms and removed the pancakes already in the frying pan, placing them on a dinner plate. There were plenty there already, with more to come. She plated up the sausages, onions, bacon, and eggs, handing a filled plate to each man. "Help yourself to pancakes." As much as she'd hated cooking back home, she didn't mind so much here. Likely because these men were appreciative of her efforts and didn't treat her like one of the soiled doves at the Welcome Saloon in Forsaken Ridge. Nor did they ogle her as though she was fair game.

Luke had seen to that, but apparently, pa didn't care either way. Besides, these were decent, law-abiding men, and she expected nothing less from them.

"Do you have any plans today," Luke asked as he was about to devour another mouthful of food.

She screwed up her nose. "Laundry mostly. It's a nice day, and there's a warm breeze." He nodded but said no more. Not that he'd said as much, but Luke had ensured at least one of the men was nearby. Ever since Sheriff Dunn had confirmed her worst fears, he'd become more protective than before, if that was even possible. She'd felt eyes on her the very next day as she'd gone to the hen house to collect the eggs. With her keen sense of self-preservation, Sarah had spotted Hank spying on her from the barn. It was all she could do not to chuckle. Not that it was a laughing matter, but the fact Luke thought she wouldn't see his spies tickled her funny bone.

All that said, their existence made her feel more comfortable about the situation. Jarrod had still appeared from time to time but didn't stay long enough for anyone to detain him. The sheriff had ridden out to the ranch a few times now, but Jarrod was nowhere to be seen on each occasion. It irritated Sarah no end.

After the kitchen was again clean and tidy, she prepared to do the laundry. The pot of water was on the stove, and she'd already grated the soap. The bed had been stripped, and she'd carried the sheets out to the laundry. Now all she had to do was wait for the water to boil. While she waited, Sarah made a batch of muffins using fresh blueberries from their garden. It had taken some time to get the garden back to a usable condition, but it had been worth it. She'd found many hidden gems, such as blueberries, carrots, and potatoes. They had all reaped the benefits of her hard work.

Since the last sighting of Jarrod, the men made a point of at least half of them coming to the house for a morning break. She was certain it was Luke's doing and would be his way of checking on her, even if he couldn't always be there himself. But, of course, he denied it, saying they all enjoyed her cooking far too much. She always sent enough muffins back for those who missed out.

She carried the heavy pot out to the laundry and, using the long stick used by Luke's mother, stirred the sheets until she was confident they were clean. Once all the excess water was gone, she carried the basket of washing to the rope between the house and laundry, all the time scanning the surrounding area.

With the last of the laundry finally hanging on the clothesline, Sarah stood back, admiring her handiwork. She loved the smell and feel of clean sheets on the bed, and today the weather was so nice; they would be dry in no time. Leaning down to pick up the now empty basket, she spotted him.

Jarrod Black stood there not ten feet away, arrogance written all over his face. "Hello Sarah," he slurred. "I love you, Sarah. Are you ready to marry me yet?"

Her heart thudded in her chest. He had become complacent, moving closer every time he visited. Did Jarrod think she was alone right now? The tip of Hank's rifle slowly came into view from the barn. And knowing she was safe, Sarah willed her heart to slow. "What do you want, Jarrod? Go away and leave me alone." She began to turn away, hoping he would leave, but it wasn't to be. He stepped even closer.

"Back off, Black," Hank called out, now showing himself to the wanted man. "I will shoot you," he said confidently. Sarah had no doubt about Hank's intentions.

Instead of doing as he was told, Jarrod moved even closer, a smug look on his face. "You and what army?" he demanded, his eyes never leaving Sarah's face.

Without further warning, Hank shot at Jarrod. For the first time, she noticed the pistol that had been in Jarrod's hand. It was now on the ground, and Jarrod's hand was bleeding. The fury on his face was palpable. "This isn't over," he ground out as he backed away, at the same time trying to stem the flow of blood. "I will be back." He stooped down to snatch up his pistol, and Hank shot at him again. Jarrod fled empty-handed and didn't look back.

Sarah had absolutely no doubt the fool would return.

Hank stood his ground and watched carefully until Jarrod was completely out of sight. "Are you all right, Missus?" He was soon by her side.

Sarah, shaking and hands clasped over her chest, nodded. Her heart was pounding, and her palms were sweaty. She'd never been so scared in her life, except perhaps when Jarrod had kidnapped her. That had been pretty terrifying. "I, I think so," she said quietly. "I'm certainly not hurt, just…scared." She hated to admit it and fought back the tears that threatened to fall. He'd taken her by surprise. Otherwise, Sarah wouldn't have been affected so much, she was certain.

But that was the way Jarrod worked–it was how he'd managed to kidnap her too. Sneaking up and grabbing her unawares. She suddenly felt light-headed at the thought; what if he managed to kidnap her again? She stumbled as she headed inside, and Hank was quickly by her side, offering his arm to steady her. He couldn't kidnap her again–this time it might be dire. She wouldn't allow it, and neither would Luke. She needed to sit down, allow herself to get her thoughts in order.

She glanced up as she heard the sound of horses' hooves.

Luke headed the group, and the other men followed closely behind. *Had they heard the gunshot?* That was the only explanation she could think of. Otherwise, why were they here? And running their poor horses into the ground in the process?

Luke was off his horse before it had even stopped. He rushed to her side and enveloped her in his arms, scanning the area around them. It was all too much, and a stray tear rolled down her cheek. "You're safe now," he caressed her cheek with his thumb. He turned to Hank. "Thank you. I don't know what would have happened if you hadn't been here."

Hank nodded, but didn't say a word. Sarah was grateful, too. Without him there, she might be dead now. What other explanation was there for Jarrod holding a gun on her? Until that moment, she hadn't thought it possible for him to want to *really* harm her, but now he seemed to be on a mission to kill her. It was all too much, and without warning, everything went black.

Luke stared down at his wife. She was ghostly pale, and it was all his fault. He should have been there for her. *Yes, he had a ranch to run, but wasn't that why he had workers?* Each and every one of them was capable, and Mack was a terrific foreman. He would ensure the place ran smoothly. Nothing was more important to him now than Sarah.

They might have started off on shaky ground, and that was on him. Luke had no intention of marrying and had always said he only wanted a housekeeper and cook, which was not possible. And, of course, he wanted an heir—no attachments, no emotion, and certainly no love. But everyone insisted that was not possible. He'd fought against it until it was no longer feasible, and now he did not know why he'd resisted so hard.

If he'd known then what he knew now, he would not have delayed the inevitable. But then again, he may not have ended up with his beautiful Sarah.

He reached down and held her hand, caressing it with his thumb. His heart thudded. What if Jarrod had killed her? According to Hank, the skunk had been so quiet, and neither Sarah nor Hank realized he was there until it was almost too late. That couldn't happen again. Luke wouldn't allow it to happen again. From now on, she would have someone guarding her every movement. He would put his most trustworthy man on it.

He shook himself mentally. *He* was his most trustworthy man, and he would guard his wife night and day. But Luke knew that was impossible. He couldn't guard her twenty-four hours a day–it was virtually impossible. His mind ticked over with the possibilities. Before he could ponder the problem further, Sarah groaned, then slowly opened her eyes.

"What happened," she asked, confusion all over her beautiful face.

Luke leaned in and kissed her forehead. "You fainted. Not that I'm surprised after all you endured today." She stared up into his face, and he couldn't pull his gaze away from those enticing eyes. They drew him in every time he stared at them.

She suddenly sat up. "Jarrod! Jarrod was here!"

He gently laid her down again. "I know, but he's gone now. The men searched the area, but he's long gone. There was a trail of blood as far down as the spring house. We checked inside, but he wasn't there. He probably left his horse there, out of sight."

"For someone who says he loves me, he has a strange way of showing it." The words were ground out. Sarah was clearly angry. What had her father been thinking, promising his daughter to that drunken fool? Since he'd passed on, they'd never know for sure, but Luke wondered if an exchange of money had been involved.

"I hate to ask," he hesitated for a moment, "But do you think it's possible Jarrod paid your father to marry you?" He almost cringed, knowing the outrage she would endure at his question.

Instead, she seemed incredibly calm. "I'm almost certain he did," she said quietly. "Pa ran out of drinking money. He had to get it from somewhere."

Her words pounded in his ears. Her father had sold her to this… vile creature for the price of a few beers. He couldn't even begin to imagine how that made her feel. But, he did know how it made him feel; he wasn't angry; he was furious. He felt the anger screaming from his head to his toes. If her father was around now, Luke would most certainly…

Well, if he was around now, Sarah would likely not be married to him. He took a deep breath and counted to ten, then stared down into the confused face of his wife. "Are you all right," she asked, reaching up to touch his cheek.

No, I'm not fine–I'm utterly furious with your dead father, he wanted to say, but instead, Luke smiled sweetly at her and squeezed Sarah's hand. "Of course." He leaned in and kissed her forehead again. Calmness seemed to engulf him at the simple action, and he knew it was Sarah's doing.

"Enough of this nonsense," she said, suddenly sitting on the side of the bed. "I have far too much to do. I can't lay about all day." Before he had a chance to protest, she had hurried into the kitchen. His wife was a strong woman, there was no doubt in his mind about that. Strong or not, she'd had a shock and needed to rest. Except she wouldn't listen to anyone, let alone her husband.

"Coffee is on the stove," she called to anyone who would listen. The workers were either in the kitchen waiting for orders or were outside on the porch surveying the area, ensuring Jarrod Black was long gone. Sarah pulled eight mugs out of the cupboard. One for each of the men and one for herself. "Help yourselves," this time loud enough for those outside to hear. She then placed a plate of muffins in the middle of the table. There wasn't a man there who refused such delights.

Sarah then went about her business, preparing a stew for supper. If he hadn't seen it with his own eyes, Luke would not have thought it possible. She still had to be shaken. He slid up behind her, to whisper in her ear, to make sure she was fine. She gasped at his touch, and he knew at that moment, his wife was putting on a show. She was terrified but was loathe to let it show.

Luke knew there and then he would either capture or kill Jarrod Black. Even if it was the last thing, he ever did.

Chapter Five

Luke had not returned to working the ranch since Jarrod's last visit some weeks ago. Mack appeared to be running the ranch just fine, but Sarah wasn't happy her husband had sacrificed his work to protect her. However, she was more than capable of looking after herself.

At least she thought she was, but Luke had now convinced her otherwise. The truth was, she'd let her guard down. Jarrod had become far more devious since he'd escaped from prison. She guessed he had to be to continue to elude capture. And that worried her.

On the plus side, she and Luke had spent plenty of time together. Far more time than she'd imagined they would ever achieve. With him refusing to leave her alone, he was at her side every second of every day. It was nice in some ways, but there were times she wished for some alone time. He vowed not to let that happen.

They sat on the porch, drinking coffee and watching out over the hillside. It was so peaceful out here, and it reminded her of home. She closed her eyes and could almost imagine she was back there in better times. She felt Luke's eyes on her.

"What are you thinking about?" he asked quietly.

She turned to face him. "Our ranch back home, when ma was still alive, and things were good." She swallowed hard, trying to stop her emotions from surfacing. "Before she died, Pa didn't hit the drink like he had after she'd gone. We had a thriving ranch, and although we weren't rich, they had each other, and there was money to spare." She stared at him, wanting him to understand. "Pa was a good man back then. He loved me and ma, and looked after us like the loving father he once was. Unfortunately, everything went awry once ma was gone."

A tear rolled down her cheek and Luke wiped it away. Since Jarrod's visit, she had felt melancholy. The slightest thing upset her, and she knew it was due to Jarrod. She wanted things to go back to the way they once were. She and Luke were happy together and had a mutual admiration for each other. Love might not have come into it, but things were *pleasant* between them. Over the time she'd been here, been married to him, Sarah had come to love Luke. Unfortunately, he'd displayed no such emotion, so she'd refrained from voicing her thoughts. Sure, he held her like he cared, and he protected her as though she mattered, but not once had he said anything that made her think he might have even an inkling of feelings for her.

No, it was better to keep quiet than to look like a fool.

She leaned back in the chair and pulled herself together, then gulped down the last of her coffee. "I must attend to lunch," she said as she stood, but light-headedness hit her the moment she was on her feet.

Luke was instantly by her side. His grip was so tight, she knew there was no possibility of her falling. "Sarah?" She knew what he was asking—*what just happened?* She didn't answer, couldn't answer, because she had no idea herself.

"I'm all right," she finally responded once her head stopped spinning. He stared at her, still unsure, but eased his grip. She hurried toward the kitchen to make the biscuits they would have with the thick vegetable soup she'd made earlier today using fresh home-grown produce. It wouldn't be long, and the men would arrive, and they'd all sit down together. She looked forward to their time together every day. The fellowship with these God-fearing men warmed her heart. They'd all been there for her on that terrible day and had been there ever since. If she were honest with herself, Sarah would admit they'd always supported her – from the moment she'd been introduced to them.

Despite the angst and the uncertainty, like clockwork, they all congregated around the big tree in the front pasture for an informal service most Sunday mornings. They aimed to go into town once a month and attend the service there, but it was far too much to attend every week.

If she was honest with herself, Sarah enjoyed those informal services. They took turns to do a reading each time and recited the Lord's Prayer. She was skeptical at first, but now she looked forward to those times.

She suddenly pulled herself out of her thoughts as the front door slammed. The biscuits would be almost ready, and she stirred the soup one last time before filling bowls with the steaming broth. With everyone cleaned up and seated around the table, she placed a bowl in front of each man and the nicely browned biscuits in the center of the table, along with some butter.

As Sarah sat, they all bowed their heads, and Luke said the blessing. "Bless this food, Father, and the people around this table. Please keep everyone safe. Amen." Everyone lifted their heads and glanced her way. These men were absolute gentlemen. They never ate until she began. It amused her, and yet she respected every one of them.

She reached for a biscuit and began to butter it. The others did the same. She felt more at home here amongst these men than she ever did with Pa's cowpokes. Luke's workers were family. Warmth spread through her at the thought. She couldn't believe that she would feel so comfortable and so wanted as she did now in the short space of a few months. Luke reached out and squeezed her hand. "The food is delicious. Thank you." A tingle went down her spine, and she wondered if he'd felt it too.

"Thanks, Missus," Colt said, followed by Roy, Pete, and Hank. The others joined in once their mouths were empty.

"You are very welcome," she said brightly. Her spirits had suddenly been lifted, and Sarah hoped it was a sign of good things to come.

Sarah lay in bed, Luke's arms wrapped around her. Despite her earlier misgivings about whether he felt love for her, Sarah's heart was filled with love, while at the same time, she was filled with dread about their future. She'd not yet convinced Luke to leave her alone and go back to his work, nor had she convinced him to let her ride with the men. Perhaps it was for the best. If Jarrod knew she was alone, he was more likely to come back and try to abduct her, or worse, kill her. At least that's what the Jarrod she knew would do. This version of Jarrod was more desperate, more uncaring than the man she'd met when she was only a teen.

That was before he'd become her father's drinking partner.

She snuggled up close against him, and Luke's warmth flooded her. He was a good man, one she would happily spend the rest of her life with. Mrs. Crookshank from the *Western Mail Order Brides Agency Mail-Order Matrimonial Agency* certainly knew how to match brides with potential husbands. Perhaps she should drop the woman a letter, let her know how she was getting on, and thank her. Luke's arm tightened around her waist, and he kissed her shoulder.

"Good morning, sleepyhead," he said, his voice husky.

She opened the eyes she'd kept closed until now, hoping sleep would overcome her once more. Sarah hadn't slept well since Jarrod had come back into her life, and she was certain Luke was the same. The black rings under their eyes proved that. "Good morning to you, too," she replied, far more brightly than she felt. Most mornings now, Sarah experienced nausea upon waking, and it became worse while she cooked breakfast. It was all she could do to keep from emptying her stomach each morning.

Luke's fingers splayed across her stomach, and suddenly he stilled. *Had he guessed her secret?* Nothing had been confirmed, so she hadn't said a word–not to Luke or anyone. He gently rolled her to face him, a grin on his face. "You've put on some weight." He studied her face but didn't say another word.

She raised her eyebrows. "So have you, along with all the workers, now that you are all eating better."

"That might be so, but…."

"Are you insinuating I'm fat?" She wore a mock scowl, and his grin vanished. She burst into laughter, and he looked confused. Sarah stared into his handsome face. Of course, he had a right to know, but she'd hoped to wait a little longer before making it official. She reached up and flicked back his overgrown black hair and stared into his chocolate brown eyes. "I…" Now that she was about to say the words, she wasn't convinced about how he would take the news.

He leaned forward and kissed her gently. "Yes?" He waited in anticipation.

"I believe I am with child," she blurted, and her heart fluttered. She was having Luke's baby, and she couldn't be happier.

"We're going to have a baby?" He suddenly drew in a deep breath, and she wasn't sure what to think. Then his grin appeared, almost splitting his face. "I'm going to be a father? I'm going to be a father!"

"Of course, I haven't seen the doctor to have it confirmed, but I'm pretty sure…."

Abruptly he threw back the covers and laid his head on her belly. "Hello, baby. I'm your Pa," he said quietly, then lifted his head and grinned at her again. Then he jumped out of bed. "Right," he looked around the room. "What should I do? You stay there, and I'll…" He stopped talking as though he had no idea what to do now that his moment of elation was over.

Sarah sat up and laughed, then slid around to sit on the side of the bed. "I'm perfectly fine. I'm pregnant, not an invalid." She stood to prove her words but quickly fell back onto the bed. Luke rushed to her side, trying to force her back into bed. "I stood up too fast, is all," she said, determined to get up again.

Luke held both her hands, ensuring she was steady this time. Once he was certain, he pulled her close against him. "I love you, Sarah," he whispered, and he sounded like he meant it, but his timing was poor. *Why did he say it now? Minutes after she'd announced she was carrying his baby?* It made

Sarah wonder if that was the only reason he'd said the words she'd longed to hear all these months.

"I love you too," she whispered, knowing that she meant every word.

"I have something to tell you," Luke said at breakfast when everyone was seated around the table. His workers all stared at him in anticipation. Sarah wanted to wait to share the news, but he was far too excited for that. "We're having a baby. I will finally have an heir."

Cheers went up, and congratulations and slaps on the back followed. When he glanced across at Sarah, she seemed deflated. He knew she was happy about the baby–she'd told him as much herself. So why did she look so unhappy? He'd said little, so it couldn't have been something he'd said. *Could it?* Luke thought back to his words, and it hit him with a thud. *Did she think he was only excited because she would give him an heir?* That would be foolish if it were the case. He loved her and had done so almost from the moment they'd met. Perhaps he should have voiced his thoughts far earlier, but he wasn't like that. It had been a stretch for him to say it out loud this morning, but the time was right, and she needed to know his true feelings.

He joined her at the countertop where she was pouring coffee and wrapped his arms around her.

"Do you know how special you are to me," he whispered. She glanced up at him, her eyes opened wide, and studied him. Then, she leaned into his chest. Luke caressed her cheek. *How could she not know how much she meant to him?*

It was totally his fault, and he vowed to ensure it didn't happen again. Without warning, she pulled out of his arms and ran outside. Luke followed her to find Sarah retching. He rubbed a hand across her back, trying to ease her discomfort.

All he wanted to do right now was hold her close and tell her everything was going to be all right. Instead, he glanced up and could have sworn he saw someone standing on the hill in the distance. He was gone as quickly as he had appeared.

His heart sank. Jarrod Black had returned.

Doctor Walter Thomas stood back after he'd finished examining Sarah. "She's with child for certain," the doc said, "But I can't be sure when it's due."

Luke had insisted on being in the examination room, which annoyed the doc, but he wasn't prepared to take any chances. Knowing Jarrod had resurfaced was more than a little disheartening. He hadn't told Sarah yet as he didn't want to worry her but knew he would have to do it. And soon. He planned to visit the sheriff before they left town.

He helped her down and waited while she straightened her clothing. "Thanks, Doc."

"You come back here in about four weeks for a checkup, Mrs. Carson," he told Sarah.

"Yes, Doctor," she answered but sounded a little uncertain. Luke would ensure she did. He wasn't prepared to put either Sarah or the baby at risk.

They stepped out onto the boardwalk, and she let out a long breath. "I'm glad that's finally over. At least now we know for sure." She turned to Luke and grinned, and his heart fluttered. How was it that a simple smile sent his heart into a tailspin? He'd dated women in the past, but none of them had ever made him feel the things Sarah did. He felt like the luckiest man in the world and knew he was.

He crooked his arm, and she slid her arm through his. "We'll go to the mercantile first," he said, knowing he had to tell her the disappointing news soon. He would delay as long as possible and let her bask in happiness while she could.

Arthur and Florence Maddison stood behind the well-used wooden counter. "Morning Flo, Arthur," Luke said cordially. "Sarah has some shopping to do, and we need to order some maternity clothes too." He glanced across at his wife, who had turned beet red at his words. She also looked quite annoyed at him and suddenly headed to the back of the store. She should be safe here, but he didn't want her to be alone, so he scurried after her.

"Congratulations," Flo called after them. Luke nodded but was more concerned about keeping Sarah safe.

Flo was suddenly by his side with a large box. "I guess you'll need this," she said as she handed it over. "Are you experiencing morning sickness," she asked Sarah gently.

Sarah nodded. "It's wearing her down," Luke answered for her.

Flo scurried off but returned a short time later, handing Sarah a large piece of ginger. "Grate it, and make tea with it. Best thing ever for morning sickness," the mother of six said cordially. "Of course, my lot are all grown now, but I don't know how I would have coped without my ginger tea during my confinements."

"Thank you, Flo," Sarah said quietly. "I really hope it helps."

Flo studied her carefully. "You look tired, dear. Use the ginger and get plenty of rest." She turned to Luke. "I'm counting on your to look after your wife." She playfully punched him on the arm, then left them alone.

The moment Flo was out of earshot, Sarah turned on him. "Why did you do that? Tell them I'm pregnant. I am so embarrassed," she whispered.

He couldn't help but laugh. "Because you will need maternity clothes, and soon. Flo will get the catalog ready for you." He reached out and pulled her close. "I'm so happy, Sarah. More than I've been in my entire life." He leaned in and kissed her forehead. "It's all because of you."

She glanced up at him then, her eyebrows close together. *Did she not believe him?* "Truthfully?"

How could she not know how he felt about her? He reached down and held her hand, then brought it to his lips. A tingle went down his spine. "Yes, truthfully. You are more important to me than anything else." He watched as a shudder went through her, then suddenly, she turned away.

She gathered flour, sugar, oats, coffee, crackers, honey, and other staple items, placing them in the box along the way. She reached for fragrant soap but changed her mind, so Luke added it anyway. When they arrived back at the front counter, she ordered milk, butter, and cream. Their one milking cow wasn't nearly enough for their requirements. Luke thought about getting another cow, but now that Sarah was pregnant, he wasn't willing to take the risk. Daisy was a placid old girl, and his wife had been milking her, but he wouldn't know about a new addition. No, he would rather pay for the extra requirements than take the risk.

He helped Sarah pick out maternity clothes from the mercantile catalog, as she'd been reluctant, but nothing was too good for his wife. In her usual way, she didn't want him spending his hard-earned money, but what else was he to do with it? Of course, when the baby came along, they would have some additional expenses, but they were sailing along nicely. In fact, he was building a nice nest egg. Money really was no object for Luke, and he wanted to spoil his wife.

He loaded their purchases into the wagon, then headed across the road to the diner for lunch. He would tell her about Jarrod after they'd eaten. The last thing Luke wanted to do was spoil her entire day. Sarah seemed particularly delighted today, and he didn't blame her, but he was certain that would change once she heard the news.

As they crossed the road, he felt eyes on him and glanced up. There was Jarrod Black–leaning casually against the butcher shop. It was as if he was saying, 'you can't get rid of me'. Luke hoped that wasn't true. He hurried Sarah inside before she spotted the fugitive.

Sarah ordered a thick vegetable soup with hot crusty bread, Luke ordered a steak and vegetables. He felt bad since his wife was still experiencing horrendous morning sickness and could not eat much, but she seemed happy enough. The doc said the morning sickness should ease up soon–he sure hoped so.

She sipped at the ginger tea she'd ordered. Hopefully Flo's home remedy worked. He'd even picked up some extra pieces to ensure she had plenty until they came to town again.

Sarah ate slowly, but Luke scoffed his food down. He sat his wife with her back to the window, but he had a full view of the goings-on outside. As though he was purposely trying to taunt him, Jarrod had stood outside the diner where Luke could see him clearly. Fury built up inside of Luke at the audacity of the man, but he was determined not to show Sarah his anger. He wanted her to enjoy her day for as long as possible.

He ordered two pieces of apple pie with clotted cream to finish off their lunch. He wanted to spoil his wife as an informal celebration of the pending birth, and Jarrod Black would not destroy that.

When they'd finished eating, Luke paid for their meal, and they left the diner. "There's something I have to tell you," he spoke softly, glancing about, "I…I have to visit the Sheriff's Office." He turned to face her, but she had a smile on her face. He was sure that would be gone in record time once he told her about Jarrod. He reached over and squeezed her hand. "I don't know how to tell you, so I'll just come out and say it." He brought her hand to his lips and kissed it.

"Jarrod's back," she said before he could utter another word.

Luke stared at her. "How did you…?"

"I'm not blind, Luke. I saw him out in the paddock yesterday."

"You didn't say anything," he said, feeling somewhat deflated.

She raised her eyebrows at him. "Neither did you." Her words were far from accusing; it was Sarah making a statement, nothing more. "I told you Jarrod was determined. The only way to rid ourselves of him is for him to go back to prison."

"There's another alternative," Luke said, staring into her face as he spoke. Of course, Sarah wouldn't want the man dead, but fugitives were often determined not to go back to prison, and then there was no other choice. Preferably not by Luke's hand or that of any of his men. And certainly not from Sarah. She would never recover from it, he was certain.

"Not that," she shook her head, her eyes filling with tears. "He was a good person in his earlier days– before he became a drunk." He watched as the color left her face. "He thinks he loves me," she said quietly. She swallowed hard, and Luke knew they had to catch him and hand the skunk over to the sheriff. All this stress couldn't be good for Sarah or the baby, and he had to find a way to capture the lowdown varmint before it was too late.

Luke put his arm around Sarah's shoulders, pulling her close. "It will be all right, I promise." He kissed her forehead, and she sunk into him. His arms came up around her, and he could have stood there all day like that.

The sound of a door opening interrupted him and the booming voice he'd come to know. "If you two have come to see me, you'd better come inside," the sheriff said, glancing about.

Sarah was shaking, and Luke had no idea how to fix it. So he led her inside, where they updated Sheriff Dunn on the latest news about Jarrod.

Chapter Six

The sheriff walked back to the wagon with them. "I cannot believe the audacity of the man," he said, shaking his head. "I've never come across someone so determined." He reached out and shook hands with Luke. "You keep this little lady safe."

Luke nodded. "Of course," he said, and Sarah wanted to throttle them both. She was ready to scream at the top of her voice that she was more than capable of defending herself.

"You do know I've shot the miserable varmint in the past, right? So I *can* look after myself." She glared at the sheriff without thinking.

Sheriff Dunn glanced up at Luke momentarily, then turned his attention to Sarah. "Nonetheless, you let the menfolk take care of you. Especially in your condition."

She wanted to yell and stomp her feet, she was so angry. Luke must have sensed how she was feeling as he reached for her hand and held it tight. "I'll make sure she's well looked after, Sheriff. Thanks for everything."

He then helped her up onto the wagon. She was filled with rage–not once did Luke defend her. She took a deep breath and counted to twenty because ten simply wasn't enough. "I'll bet I can shoot better than the sheriff," she ground out, and Luke chuckled.

"I know," he said. "But he doesn't know that. Just be grateful everyone is looking out for you." He jumped aboard and pulled her close. "How are you feeling?"

She rested her head on his shoulder. "I think the ginger tea has helped. I don't feel anywhere near as queasy as I have been." It was a blessed relief. At least for now. *God sent these things to try us,* she thought, *and this is no different.* Apart from the morning sickness, Sarah felt good. Food had been scarce back home, and she had eaten much better since she'd married Luke and come to Carson's Hollow to live. She also slept far better than she did at home. Likely because she had a mattress stuffed with hay back home in Forsaken Ridge. Luke had a feather mattress, which was the height of luxury for her, much like the one at the *Homestead Inn.* She was very grateful Mrs. Crookshank had insisted she stay there. Knowing Luke as she did now, he would probably be horrified she'd even booked herself into Woody's sleazy saloon, let alone stayed there before Mrs. Crookshank had arrived on the scene.

As Luke flicked the reins for the horses to go, Sarah saw something out of the corner of her eye. It moved so swiftly she had no idea if it was Jarrod or not. If she had to guess, she'd say yes. Her heart pounded. They were sitting ducks out here and needed to hurry home. She reached down to ensure the rifle was still there, and it was. She felt relief but knew their ordeal was not over. Jarrod Black had far too many tricks up his sleeve to leave them alone. Sarah knew him all too well, which probably worked in their favor. If he would just slink back to where he came from, her life would be perfect.

Fortunately, or perhaps, unfortunately, she knew how determined he was. She also knew he would never leave her alone until he'd claimed her as his own. She reached down again, this time snatching up the rifle and checking it was still loaded, which it was. "Come on, you lowdown skunk," she said when they were out of town and entirely surrounded by trees. "Come on out where I can shoot you," she said under her breath. She saw the shocked expression on Luke's face but wanted this over with. Wished it was over right here and now.

Sarah knew she sounded demented, but there was nothing she could do about it. Jarrod had pushed her to the edge, and now she had to get the better of him. It was like a contest for Jarrod–he'd always reveled in the challenge. The fact of the matter was he was every bit as good a shooter as she was. In their teenage years, they would challenge each other to see who was more accurate, and they'd always come out neck and neck. The thought made her shudder.

Back then, it was a bit of fun. Now it was a fight for life: her life and that of her baby. Luke was probably also in his sights since in Jarrod's eyes, he stole Sarah from him. She had no doubt Jarrod wouldn't care if he had to kill her to win. He'd proven that the day he'd pointed his pistol at her. If Hank hadn't been around to scare him off, she wasn't sure if she'd even be alive now. The thought terrified her, not only for herself but for her unborn baby.

She suddenly drew in a deep breath at the thought. "Are you all right," Luke asked, putting a hand to her knee. She wasn't, and Sarah knew it, but she had no intention of admitting the fact. Instead, she nodded.

"There," she said suddenly as she noticed a flash between the trees. "He's behind those trees. I'm going to pick him off if it's the last thing I do." She lifted the rifle and lined it up, holding steady despite the wagon rattling along the road. "Dang it, the coward took off before I could get a clean shot."

She lowered the rifle, and Luke glanced about. "Are you sure he was there? I didn't see anything."

"Oh, he was there all right. Given the chance, I'd get a clean shot, but it wasn't meant to be today." *But I'll get him,* she decided. It had to be Sarah getting Jarrod, or he'd be sure to get her – when she least expected it.

By the time they arrived home, Sarah was exhausted. It had been a long day, and there was still a lot of it left. She began to carry their purchases inside, but Luke stopped her.

"Go inside and put your feet up," he demanded. He might not say it, but Sarah knew the truth behind his words–he didn't want her to be out in the open like a sitting duck. Jarrod was out there somewhere, she would bet her life on it. He was a coward, though, and wouldn't show himself. There was no doubt in her mind he knew he would be shot by either herself or one of the men on Luke's property. He simply wouldn't take the chance.

When she thought about it, he'd always been a coward. All those months he'd followed, harassed, and stalked her, he had kept himself hidden most of the time. She was taken by surprise when he'd kidnapped her, not only because she didn't hear him coming but also because it meant he had to show himself in town with her trussed up like a Thanksgiving turkey.

That's what she'd like to do to him right now. Truss him up and present the lowdown varmint to the sheriff, who would ship him right back to prison. Only this time, he would have a far longer sentence. Not that she'd seen it back then, but looking back now, he'd always been this way. Pa had always talked him up for as long as Sarah could remember. It made her wonder if the two had planned for Jarrod to marry her–even all those years ago.

It was yet another reason for her to think badly of her pa. It brought a tear to her eye–when ma was around, he was a loving father. She never would have guessed he'd turn to drink after ma's untimely death.

Trying to take her mind off sadder times, she poked at the woodstove and ensured the kettle was full. The men had arrived back at the ranch house and would surely want coffee. She'd made oat cookies yesterday and would serve them up for afternoon tea. Since they'd been out all day, she hadn't had the time to bake today. Sarah knew she was spoiling the men, but since Luke wouldn't allow her to work the ranch, she had to fill in her time somehow. Of course, once the baby arrived, it would be a different story, but she would have liked to do something at least a little useful.

It was too late now. She was with child, and there was no way Luke would let her ride or help out in any way. She wasn't even able to milk old Daisy. Since he'd discovered her condition, he refused to allow her to do that. It was something Sarah had always enjoyed, and strangely enough, found it rather relaxing. Her husband thought she was crazy–it was a job he hated.

Colt strolled through the front door, carrying a large box. "Put it on the table, please," she requested. Luke had obviously directed the men to bring in their purchases. Unpacking and stacking the pantry was not a job she envied.

One by one, boxes of goods were brought inside. Finally, she added the perishable items to the root cellar. Sarah wasn't certain the spring house would ever get used again. There must have been a time it was used. It got her to thinking Luke's grandfather must have employed a lot of workers back then. Otherwise, why would it have been built to begin with?

She brought her mind back to the task at hand and began preparing coffee. The rest of the unpacking could wait. None of it would spoil. She placed the filled mugs on the table, then reached up to pull a tin of cookies from a high shelf in the cupboard. Luke was behind her in record time. "I'll do that. I don't want you reaching up like that." He pulled the tin down and placed it on the countertop, then his hands slipped around her belly.

Sarah leaned back into him, reveling in his nearness. How did she get so lucky? He leaned down and kissed her neck. A tingle went down her spine. She turned in his arms and glanced up at him. He looked so happy. Was he pleased because of the baby, or because of her, or perhaps the two combined? Either way, Sarah was the happiest she'd been for a very long time. "I have to dish out the cookies," she whispered.

"I don't want to let you go," he whispered back, then picked up the tin of cookies and placed them in the middle of the table. The workers obviously didn't care because they were soon reaching in to take them.

She rested her head against his shoulder. "I could stay here all day." Sarah knew she could. Luke was special, and he made her feel comfortable, loved, and protected all at the same time. *What would she do if Jarrod decided the best way to get to her was to kill Luke?* The thought made her heart thud, then her heart rate suddenly kicked up, making her light-headed. Dark thoughts flooded her very being. She asked herself if Jarrod would do that? Sarah knew he would do it in a heartbeat if it meant getting his way of claiming Sarah as his own. Before long, she felt herself sliding down Luke's body and into the abyss.

Voices surrounded her. They seemed to come from far away, and Sarah had no idea where she was or how she got there. Had Jarrod finally got to her?

She felt a gentle hand caressing her cheek. "Sarah." She opened her eyes slowly, not certain she wanted to open them. The voice echoed in her head, and she couldn't make it out or who it belonged to. "Sarah, it's Luke."

Her breath came whooshing out in relief. She stared up at him and almost cried. She was so happy to see him there. "What happened?"

Luke stared down at her and reached for her hand. "You fainted. I have no idea why except maybe because you're pregnant?"

It all came flooding back, and her eyes filled with tears. "I don't want Jarrod to kill you!" She almost shouted and couldn't stop herself from sobbing. Luke handed her a handkerchief, and she wiped at her leaking eyes. Sarah was not one to cry under normal circumstances, but nothing was normal right now.

Luke stared at her in disbelief, then his brows crinkled with confusion. "Kill me? That's absurd." He lifted her hand and squeezed it. When he did that, she always felt reassured, but not this time.

She sat up. "He's out there, waiting and watching. If he can't get to me, he'll kill you to make it easier for him."

Luke pulled her closer and caressed her back. "He won't get to either of us, so don't worry your pretty little head over it."

"You don't know him like I do," she whispered, then buried her head in his chest. Jarrod could be outside right now, stalking them as he'd done to her in Forsaken Ridge. She would put nothing past him. Nothing at all.

Sarah made chicken pot pie for supper. It was fairly quick and easy to do, and the men all loved it. There was a pot of potatoes on the stove and fresh beans from the garden. Cooking kept her busy and being busy kept her mind off her troubles. She was sure trouble was lurking outside somewhere, watching her every move.

Did he realize she was with child? More likely than not, he didn't. It might be enough to have him turn on her—carrying another man's baby would not sit well with Jarrod. Even teenage Jarrod would not have been thrilled with that prospect, and it filled Sarah with dread. She reached for a chair and sat down to catch her breath. This was a scenario she hadn't thought about before.

Truth be told, she shouldn't have to think about such things. She should be enjoying her time as a mother-to-be, making plans for cribs, diapers, and baby clothes. Not trying to find ways to stay alive. She rubbed her hands across her belly and tried to calm herself down.

Luke strolled in from outside with a bucket of wood and kindling. He stopped in his tracks as he noticed her. "Everything all right?"

By now, Sarah knew she couldn't hide anything from him, but she would try anyway. "Just taking a quick break."

He stared at her, seemingly unconvinced, but continued to the stove where he deposited the bucket. Opening the stove, he poked at the wood already burning and added some more pieces. He glanced up at the loaf of bread sitting on the countertop and leaned over it, taking in its aroma. "You have done far too much today," he admonished, and she shrugged.

"It's not that much. I'm pregnant, not an invalid." He frowned at her, and Sarah understood Luke thought they were one and the same. He opened his mouth to respond, but before he could say another word, the men poured through the front door. Mack stopped as he noticed the two huddled in the kitchen and indicated for the others to do the same. One thing Sarah could categorically say is the men always gave them their privacy. They never infringed on their private conversations and never knowingly eavesdropped. For that, she was very thankful.

She stood to finish preparing supper, and the men proceeded into the kitchen, where they took their places. Luke carried the pie out of the oven, and the aroma filled the room. For once it didn't send Sarah running outside. The ginger tea seemed to be doing its job. She would be forever grateful to Flo for the information.

Luke drained the pot of potatoes while Sarah drained the beans. She dished out the food and placed a plate in front of every man. The loaf of bread was also placed on the table, along with a large knife. Sarah took her place, and they all joined hands.

"Lord, bless this food and these people. Amen." Luke held onto her hand after the blessing was said and seemed reluctant to let go.

Amen echoed around the table, and finally he dropped her hand. "This is delicious," he said after the first mouthful.

"It certainly is," Pete said.

"Yep," said Roy, who never said much to anyone.

"Oh, my rice pudding will be ready!" Sarah began to stand, but Luke beat her to it.

"I'll get it," he said, and that's precisely what he did. She had no idea how she'd managed to get such a wonderful man who was so caring and looked after her no matter what. The scent of the pudding added to all the delicious smells drifting around her kitchen. It reminded her of when her mother was still alive and spending her days baking. Sarah felt blessed to have experienced that, as she knew many who never did. "Smells good." Luke's voice came out of nowhere, bringing her back to the present. She smiled, but didn't say a word. "You really do spoil us," he said, taking his seat at the table again.

It was Luke who spoiled her. Sarah had never felt so wanted in her entire life. When she was younger, she had felt that way, but not to the extent of now. It was as though she'd found her calling in life. Never in her wildest dreams did she think becoming someone's wife would fulfill her the way it had. It made her realize that wanting to help out on the ranch was more out of habit than desire. She'd been working her father's ranch before she was even a teenager and knew nothing else.

Suddenly, she was on high alert. "Someone is outside," she said urgently, then rushed toward the closet where the rifle was kept. Luke was right behind her and took the rifle out of her trembling hands. Did he think she was trigger happy? Well, he was probably right. Unfortunately, she was when it came to Jarrod.

"Go back to the kitchen," he said quietly, then opened the front door gingerly.

His hand ready to knock, Sheriff McKenzie Dunn stood at the door. He frowned when he saw the rifle in Luke's hands. "Sheriff! Come on in." Luke placed the firearm back in the closet, then led the sheriff to the table. "We were just eating. Come and join us."

Everyone shuffled along to make room for the town's long-time sheriff, and Sarah dished out a serving for him, even while he protested. The man had to be hungry–it was an hour's ride to the Carson's Hollow Ranch. "Thank you, Mrs. Carson. I didn't mean to put you to any trouble."

"No trouble, Sheriff. There's always plenty to go round." She poured him a coffee and placed it in front of him. "Help yourself to bread. Freshly baked today. And please, call me Sarah."

"Well, thank you, Mrs. er, Sarah. I do appreciate it." He took a few mouthfuls of the food, saying how good it was, then turned to Luke. "I have news, but perhaps it should wait until after supper."

Sarah's heart fluttered. *What news? Was it good or bad?* She wanted so badly for Luke to convince the sheriff to tell them now.

"Sounds good. Enjoy your meal, and we'll talk later." Her heart sunk. Why couldn't they just get it over and done with now? But she knew the reason. They didn't want to spoil anyone's supper. Would this nightmare ever end? The way she felt right now, Sarah didn't think so.

Chapter Seven

Jarrod was here; Sarah knew he was. He was probably lurking outside right now. The thought sent a shudder coursing through her.

It didn't take a genius to guess the sheriff's news was bad. If it had been good, he would have blurted it out when he walked through the door. She glanced at Luke. Had he come to the same conclusion? He looked far more serious than he had a few minutes ago.

"That would have to be the best meal I've had in a very long time," Sheriff Dunn said, patting his stomach after finishing a serve of rice pudding. "But don't tell Jeannie at the diner. She'd skin me alive." He chuckled, and the others joined him.

"What you need, Sheriff, is a mail-order bride." At first the sheriff chuckled at Luke's words, but Sarah noted he became contemplative once he realized Luke meant every word.

"I don't think so," Sheriff Dunn said. "How do you even get yourself a mail-order bride? I wouldn't know where to start."

"I was a mail-order bride," Sarah offered. "I was dubious at first, but as you know, I was left with little choice."

"Best thing I ever did," Luke interjected, and his words sent warmth flooding through her.

"Well, in that case, it's something to consider."

"More coffee, Sheriff? Anyone?" Sarah asked, holding up the pot. She knew she was putting off the inevitable, but if it was bad news, as she was confident it was, she wasn't certain she wanted to hear it.

"Thank you, Sarah," he said, holding out his mug.

"Shall we move into the sitting room where it's more comfortable," Luke suggested, making a statement rather than asking a question. The men all snatched up their refilled mugs and moved to the other room. "Are you coming, Sarah? I'm sure this involves you."

"It does," the sheriff said as he nodded. Sarah studied him. She'd not taken a lot of notice before, but now she saw he was a big man. He was every bit as tall as Luke but was far more solid and all muscle. He wore two guns, and Sarah felt somewhat reassured. She still wasn't convinced he was as good a shot as she was, but that was beside the point.

Luke sat down, pulling her onto his lap. At first, she felt annoyed, but then realized with everyone there, seating was limited. His arms crept up and around her belly, and she felt somewhat reassured her baby was safe in his hands.

"I won't beat around the bush. Jarrod Black was seen heading this way."

She stared at the sheriff. "I knew it. I saw the lowdown varmint when we were coming back from town. Would have shot him too if I'd been able to get a clean shot."

Sheriff Dunn chuckled as though he thought it was a joke. When no one else laughed, he glanced at Luke for confirmation. "She did try," Luke said. "But he got away. More's the pity."

Sarah stared at the sheriff in disbelief. "You didn't believe me when I said I'd shot him before." She silently counted to ten before speaking again. "You all need to understand," she pointed from one man to another, "That Jarrod and me practiced shooting together from a young age. He's a crack shot, just like me. Only he's a drunkard now, which probably makes him far more dangerous."

You could have split the air with a knife. The silence was deafening, and the men all looked at each other for reassurance. "You don't believe me? Do I have to prove myself?"

Luke's hands tightened around her. "I don't think it's that. I think everyone is stunned to find out you and Jarrod were such good friends."

"Yeah, we were once. But clearly not anymore. Since my pa died, the lowdown skunk has kidnapped, harassed, and now tried to kill me. All because he wants to marry me. He's no friend of mine." She almost spat the words; she was so angry.

Sarah stared out the window. It was pitch black outside. "Sheriff, you should stay tonight. If Jarrod is hanging around, it's too dangerous to go back to town in the dark."

Luke backed her up. "I agree. You already risked your life to come here and warn us. We have a spare bed, and you're very welcome to stay. Sarah cooks a mean breakfast too."

"In that case, how can I refuse," McKenzie said. "Thank you both. I will take up your generous offer."

Sarah left the men to talk amongst themselves while she saw to the dishes and cleaned up the kitchen. She felt far more reassured knowing the sheriff was here, along with Luke and his workers. If only they could catch Jarrod and ship him back off to jail. She would feel far less anxious.

"I'm going to check outside before bed," Luke whispered. If he thought Sarah couldn't hear him, he was sadly mistaken.

"I'll come with you," Sheriff Dunn said. "I need to see to my horse as well."

The pair went outside, and everyone else dispersed to the bunkhouse, leaving Sarah alone inside.

The door closed noisily behind the men, and Sarah breathed a sigh of relief. It felt like forever since she'd been alone for more than a minute or two. She finished tidying the kitchen and straightened the chairs, then prepared the bread for the morning, setting it aside on the countertop to rise overnight.

She thought she had enough eggs for breakfast but decided to check the pantry. Even if there weren't enough there, the chickens would have laid more by the time she needed them. Feeling as though a weight had been lifted due to the presence of the sheriff, she strolled happily into the pantry. There were a dozen eggs in there, so she would need to collect more before breakfast. She checked the root cellar, and found plenty of bacon, butter, and milk.

It was only a small gesture, but offering to have the sheriff stay overnight was her way of thanking him.

Besides, she didn't want him put in danger for her sake. Sarah heard the front door click and knew the men were back. She was past ready for bed and hurried back to the kitchen.

"Well, looky here," a familiar voice slurred. "My Sarah, and she's all alone for once."

Sarah shuddered at the sight of Jarrod standing there in her kitchen. "What do you want," she demanded, dredging up as much bravado as she could manage. She was trembling, but tried to hide the fact by pushing her hands into her skirt pockets. Oh, how she wished she had a small pistol in those pockets. She could end it here and now. Sadly, that was not the case, and she was in no position to physically fight Jarrod. After all, she had to think of her baby. Ordinarily, she would fight him, and although Jarrod was the stronger of the two, he was also drunk. She could smell the alcohol on him, even this far away.

She warily ran her eyes down to his hands and silently prayed for God's protection. As she suspected, he held a pistol and no doubt would shoot her at a moment's notice. The first thought that ran through her mind was to protect her baby with her hands. If she did, and he realized she was pregnant, would he shoot with the aim of killing Luke's baby? She wouldn't put it past the mongrel. As difficult as it was, she was determined not to give him the opportunity.

Distract him. She needed to distract the crazy varmint. "Would you like coffee, Jarrod," she said with as much pleasantness as she could muster. The man was abhorrent to her, but she needed to appease him, keep him happy. He stared at her for a long moment, and Sarah wondered if he was contemplating killing her.

"That would be nice. You always were a good hostess," he slurred, a sneer in his voice. She was *never* a good hostess, and they both knew it. His animosity was worrying.

As she reached into the cupboard, she remembered what Luke said about watching out for the baby and pretended she couldn't reach. "Would you mind? I can't quite reach." He stepped forward, passing her a mug. Sarah stepped back, not wanting to be too close. Apart from the fact that he reeked from weeks of not bathing, she didn't trust him one iota. "Have you eaten? I can rustle something up for you." She wanted to keep him busy, keep his mind off his intentions, and it was the only way she could think of.

She pulled a table cloth out of the drawer and placed it on the table, then set a place for him. She strategically sat him with his back to the door, hoping Luke and the sheriff would eventually come inside and rescue her. "What would you like? I have freshly baked biscuits from supper, and there's also chicken pot pie. I remember that was always your favorite," she said, not quite certain that was true.

He grinned. "You remembered. You see, we were meant for each other."

Did that cement her place in his heart? Or was he still out to kill her? Panic was working its way through her, and Sarah wasn't sure she could continue with the subterfuge. She heated the pie over a pot of boiling water and kept him distracted with talk of their past until it was hot enough to eat. She then placed it on the table in front of her unwanted guest.

"This is good," he said with his mouth full. "You always were a good cook." The way he shoveled food into his mouth, it appeared he hadn't eaten for days. Which was probably right. Being on the run the way he was likely meant he had little access to food. He wouldn't have money to buy a meal either.

She forced a smile onto her face. "I have rice pudding for dessert if you'd like some." She knew he wouldn't be able to resist. It was yet another food she knew Jarrod enjoyed.

He nodded as he shoved in another mouthful. She lifted the coffee pot, ready to refill his mug when she saw movement out of the corner of her eye. Relief flooded her as Luke, and Sheriff Dunn silently made their way through the door, guns drawn.

They crept toward their prey, keeping their existence secret until the last moment. Then, with a gun to his back, Jarrod put his hands up. "I thought you were better than this," he spat out, his words directed at Sarah.

But she was having none of it. "I thought *you* were better than this, Jarrod. But you proved how truly awful you could be. That's all on you. Everything you did to me? That was your fault. I didn't force you to do any of it. Enjoy your time in jail." She smiled at him, at the same time glaring. Finally, she turned her back to Jarrod as the sheriff handcuffed him.

"We'll secure him in the barn tonight," Luke said behind her, his voice getting closer. "Mack and Sheriff Dunn have agreed to take turns guarding him." Luke's words were reassuring, but his arms slipping around her, even more so. "There's an empty horse stall," Luke added. "I'm sure we can keep him secure there. We have plenty of spare ropes you can use. Mack knows where they are."

"You can't…." Jarrod protested, but no one seemed to care.

"We sure can," Sheriff Dunn said, then the two men marched him out to the barn.

Sarah turned in Luke's arms, relief overwhelming her now her ordeal was over. She glanced up into Luke's face, and had never been so happy to see him. Or to be held by him. He lifted a hand and caressed her face, and she molded into him. "Thank you," she mumbled. "I'm not sure I could have held him off much longer."

"You did well. It will be a very long time before Jarrod Black is released from jail now. Adding hostage-taking to his charge of kidnapping will add years to his sentence." He pulled her close and wrapped his wife in his arms. Sarah reveled in his nearness and closed her eyes, pretending, at least for now, that Jarrod hadn't held her hostage in her own home.

"What do you think will happen to him?" Sarah was relieved as they sat around the breakfast table but curious about the sentence Jarrod would likely receive.

"If I had to guess, I'd say he'll be in jail for at least ten years. Maybe even more." Sheriff McKenzie Dunn took a gulp of his coffee before speaking again. "Especially now his cousin, the judge, who is no longer a judge, by the way, is out of the picture."

Despite what he'd done to her, and knowing her relief that her ordeal was now over, Sarah felt sorry for Jarrod. Who could have predicted his life would have taken such a turn. On the other hand, she wouldn't have married Luke without his intervention, and that would be such a shame.

"More pancakes, Sheriff?"

McKenzie patted his belly. "How do you survive all this food without putting on weight," he asked Luke. "Your wife is a terrific cook. If I could get a bride who could cook as good as her, I might contemplate your mail-order bride suggestion." He chuckled.

Sarah piled more pancakes onto his plate without waiting for an answer. Sheriff Dunn tucked into everything put before him.

Four weeks later…

Luke and Sarah stood outside the courthouse and watched as Jarrod, shackled hands and feet, was placed in the jail wagon. It was a pitiful sight, and at first Sarah almost felt sorry for him, but after everything he'd put them all through, she had no sympathy left for the weasel.

The fact it had come to this was upsetting. Why couldn't he simply accept the fact she didn't want to marry him? She'd never seen him as marriage material–even when they were teenagers. He was too easy with the booze and too quick to anger. She could have almost predicted it would come to this.

A shudder ran through her at the thought. What would pa say now if he'd seen the way Jarrod had behaved? He would be so oblivious himself; he would not have been able to see the signs even if he'd still been here.

Sadness suddenly overtook her. Never in a million years did Sarah ever think she would end up in this situation. Jarrod had been such a kind boy when they were young. *Where did it all go so wrong?*

"What are you thinking?"

Luke's voice brought her out of her private thoughts, and she glanced up at him, smiling tentatively. She thanked her lucky stars for having married him. She wasn't sure what she would have done without him by her side. "A lot of things, but especially how lucky I am to be married to you." He reached down and held her hand, squeezing it gently. She suddenly brought his hand to her belly, and Luke's eyes opened wide in delight. "I think our baby is trying to say hello." She smiled, and all the worries of the past disappeared.

Luke leaned in and kissed her forehead. Sarah couldn't imagine being married to anyone else or living anywhere else. She belonged in Carson's Hollow and knew she never wanted to leave unless it was with Luke.

Epilogue

Ten months later…

Sarah and Luke walked hand in hand, the weight of the world off their shoulders. After that fateful night all those months ago, Sheriff McKenzie Dunn had become a good friend, despite the distance between them.

He'd visited only three days ago to let them know Jarrod Black was dead, killed after he'd goaded one too many prisoners. It was bound to happen, he'd said. The man was quick to anger and even quicker trying to stir up trouble. The theory was he'd done it on purpose, trying to end his life. With another ten years to serve, Jarrod was not the best of prisoners.

Sarah had prayed for his soul and that he'd finally found peace. Jarrod had lived a tortured existence for a very long time. She had tried to help him, tried to get him off the booze, along with her father, but nothing worked for either of them. Alcohol was the root of all evil as far as Sarah was concerned, and she was pleased it was not something Luke indulged in.

She squeezed his hand and smiled. Life had been good to them lately.

They strolled toward the front paddock where the horses had been grazing, and Sarah reveled in their attention. She had managed a ride here and there, but not many. After all, she'd been busy with her new baby. She reached into her pocket and pulled out pieces of apple, which were quickly snatched up. When her supplies were depleted, they began the short walk back to the ranch house, warmth and contentment filling her very soul.

She glanced up at the sound of whimpering, and they hurried back toward the porch where five-month-old baby Ethan was stirring. They stood over the crib staring down at the baby, who looked so much like his father with his jet black hair and handsome face. Sarah's heart fluttered at the love she felt for these two men in her life. She couldn't wait to meet their next creation. Their lives were filled with love for each other and their little family.

Luke turned to her and smiled. "Thank you," he said, then put a hand to her slightly swollen belly. "Maybe this one will be the girl you craved."

She looked up at him as she reached into the crib for Ethan. "Don't you know by now? It doesn't matter if it's a girl or a boy. Provided I'm here with you, and our babies are healthy, nothing else matters." Tears filled her eyes at the overwhelming love she felt at that very moment.

She silently thanked God for keeping them all safe and bringing such joy into their lives. She also prayed for more babies in the future, if that was what He also wanted.

Luke leaned in to kiss her forehead, then tickled Ethan under the chin. The baby giggled, and all was well with her world. Sarah felt tears of happiness roll down her cheeks.

The End

From the Author

Thank you so much for reading my book – I hope you enjoyed it.

I would greatly appreciate you leaving a review where you purchased, even if it is only a one-liner. It helps to have my books more visible!

If you enjoyed this book, you may like to read Sheriff McKenzie Dunn's story, A Bride for McKenzie, also by Cheryl Wright.

About the

Author

Multi-published, award-winning and bestselling author Cheryl Wright, former secretary, debt collector, account manager, writing coach, and shopping tour hostess, loves reading.

She writes both historical and contemporary western romance, as well as romantic suspense.

She lives in Melbourne, Australia, and is married with two adult children and has six grandchildren. When she's not writing, she can be found in her craft room making greeting cards.

Links:

Website: *http://www.cheryl-wright.com/*

Facebook Reader Group:
https://www.facebook.com/groups/cherylwrightaut hor/

Join My Newsletter:
https://cheryl-wright.com/newsletter/
(and receive a free book)